S0-ADQ-101

ARCTIC WINGS

SELECTED FICTION WORKS BY
L. RON HUBBARD

FANTASY
The Case of the Friendly Corpse

Death's Deputy

Fear

The Ghoul

The Indigestible Triton

Slaves of Sleep & The Masters of Sleep

Typewriter in the Sky

The Ultimate Adventure

SCIENCE FICTION
Battlefield Earth

The Conquest of Space

The End Is Not Yet

Final Blackout

The Kilkenny Cats

The Kingslayer

The Mission Earth Dekalogy*

Ole Doc Methuselah

To the Stars

ADVENTURE
The Hell Job series

WESTERN
Buckskin Brigades

Empty Saddles

Guns of Mark Jardine

Hot Lead Payoff

A full list of L. Ron Hubbard's
novellas and short stories is provided at the back.

*Dekalogy—a group of ten volumes

L. RON HUBBARD

ARCTIC WINGS

GALAXY
PRESS

Published by
Galaxy Press, LLC
7051 Hollywood Boulevard, Suite 200
Hollywood, CA 90028

© 2013 L. Ron Hubbard Library. All Rights Reserved.

Any unauthorized copying, translation, duplication, importation or distribution,
in whole or in part, by any means, including electronic copying, storage or
transmission, is a violation of applicable laws.

Mission Earth is a trademark owned by L. Ron Hubbard Library and
is used with permission. *Battlefield Earth* is a trademark owned
by Author Services, Inc. and is used with permission.

Horsemen illustration from *Western Story Magazine* is © and ™ Condé
Nast Publications and is used with their permission. Fantasy, Far-Flung Adventure
and Science Fiction illustrations: *Unknown* and *Astounding Science Fiction* copyright ©
by Street & Smith Publications, Inc. Reprinted with permission of Penny
Publications, LLC. Story Preview illustration: *Argosy Magazine* is © 1936
Argosy Communications, Inc. All Rights Reserved. Reprinted with
permission from Argosy Communications, Inc.

Printed in the United States of America.

ISBN-10 1-59212-255-8
ISBN-13 978-1-59212-255-4

Library of Congress Control Number: 2007903617

CONTENTS

STORIES FROM PULP FICTION'S GOLDEN AGE

A ND it *was* a golden age.

The 1930s and 1940s were a vibrant, seminal time for a gigantic audience of eager readers, probably the largest per capita audience of readers in American history. The magazine racks were chock-full of publications with ragged trims, garish cover art, cheap brown pulp paper, low cover prices—and the most excitement you could hold in your hands.

"Pulp" magazines, named for their rough-cut, pulpwood paper, were a vehicle for more amazing tales than Scheherazade could have told in a million and one nights. Set apart from higher-class "slick" magazines, printed on fancy glossy paper with quality artwork and superior production values, the pulps were for the "rest of us," adventure story after adventure story for people who liked to *read*. Pulp fiction authors were no-holds-barred entertainers—real storytellers. They were more interested in a thrilling plot twist, a horrific villain or a white-knuckle adventure than they were in lavish prose or convoluted metaphors.

The sheer volume of tales released during this wondrous golden age remains unmatched in any other period of literary history—hundreds of thousands of published stories in over nine hundred different magazines. Some titles lasted only an issue or two; many magazines succumbed to paper shortages during World War II, while others endured for decades yet. Pulp fiction remains as a treasure trove of stories you can read, stories you can love, stories you can remember. The stories were driven by plot and character, with grand heroes, terrible villains, beautiful damsels (often in distress), diabolical plots, amazing places, breathless romances. The readers wanted to be taken beyond the mundane, to live adventures far removed from their ordinary lives—and the pulps rarely failed to deliver.

In that regard, pulp fiction stands in the tradition of all memorable literature. For as history has shown, good stories are much more than fancy prose. William Shakespeare, Charles Dickens, Jules Verne, Alexandre Dumas—many of the greatest literary figures wrote their fiction for the readers, not simply literary colleagues and academic admirers. And writers for pulp magazines were no exception. These publications reached an audience that dwarfed the circulations of today's short story magazines. Issues of the pulps were scooped up and read by over thirty million avid readers each month.

Because pulp fiction writers were often paid no more than a cent a word, they had to become prolific or starve. They also had to write aggressively. As Richard Kyle, publisher and editor of *Argosy*, the first and most long-lived of the pulps, so pointedly explained: "The pulp magazine writers, the best of them, worked for markets that did not write for critics or attempt to satisfy timid advertisers. Not having to answer to anyone other than their readers, they wrote about human beings on the edges of the unknown, in those new lands the future would explore. They wrote for what we would become, not for what we had already been."

Some of the more lasting names that graced the pulps include H. P. Lovecraft, Edgar Rice Burroughs, Robert E. Howard, Max Brand, Louis L'Amour, Elmore Leonard, Dashiell Hammett, Raymond Chandler, Erle Stanley Gardner, John D. MacDonald, Ray Bradbury, Isaac Asimov, Robert Heinlein—and, of course, L. Ron Hubbard.

In a word, he was among the most prolific and popular writers of the era. He was also the most enduring—hence this series—and certainly among the most legendary. It all began only months after he first tried his hand at fiction, with L. Ron Hubbard tales appearing in *Thrilling Adventures, Argosy, Five-Novels Monthly, Detective Fiction Weekly, Top-Notch, Texas Ranger, War Birds, Western Stories,* even *Romantic Range.* He could write on any subject, in any genre, from jungle explorers to deep-sea divers, from G-men and gangsters, cowboys and flying aces to mountain climbers, hard-boiled detectives and spies. But he really began to shine when he turned his talent to science fiction and fantasy of which he authored nearly fifty novels or novelettes to forever change the shape of those genres.

Following in the tradition of such famed authors as Herman Melville, Mark Twain, Jack London and Ernest Hemingway, Ron Hubbard actually lived adventures that his own characters would have admired—as an ethnologist among primitive tribes, as prospector and engineer in hostile climes, as a captain of vessels on four oceans. He even wrote a series of articles for *Argosy,* called "Hell Job," in which he lived and told of the most dangerous professions a man could put his hand to.

Finally, and just for good measure, he was also an accomplished photographer, artist, filmmaker, musician and educator. But he was first and foremost a *writer,* and that's the L. Ron Hubbard we come to know through the pages of this volume.

This library of Stories from the Golden Age presents the best of L. Ron Hubbard's fiction from the heyday of storytelling, the Golden Age of the pulp magazines. In these eighty volumes, readers are treated to a full banquet of 153 stories, a kaleidoscope of tales representing every imaginable genre: science fiction, fantasy, western, mystery, thriller, horror, even romance—action of all kinds and in all places.

Because the pulps themselves were printed on such inexpensive paper with high acid content, issues were not meant to endure. As the years go by, the original issues of every pulp from *Argosy* through *Zeppelin Stories* continue crumbling into brittle, brown dust. This library preserves the L. Ron Hubbard tales from that era, presented with a distinctive look that brings back the nostalgic flavor of those times.

L. Ron Hubbard's Stories from the Golden Age has something for every taste, every reader. These tales will return you to a time when fiction was good clean entertainment and the most fun a kid could have on a rainy afternoon or the best thing an adult could enjoy after a long day at work.

Pick up a volume, and remember what reading is supposed to be all about. Remember curling up with a *great story.*

—Kevin J. Anderson

KEVIN J. ANDERSON *is the author of more than ninety critically acclaimed works of speculative fiction, including The Saga of Seven Suns, the continuation of the Dune Chronicles with Brian Herbert, and his* New York Times *bestselling novelization of L. Ron Hubbard's* Ai! Pedrito!

ARCTIC WINGS

CHAPTER ONE

SPRING had come to White Bear Landing and for three days the Tokush River, which emptied into the lake and poured forth again, had clogged the waters with broken trees and brush.

But this was not the only flotsam which the Tokush brought out of the unmapped, white reaches of the Arctic. Spring brought back the game, and following the game came the carnivores, the wolves and Taggart.

The lake was blue as the sky, and the trees were green, and a crystal sweetness was in the air, and on the porch of the White Bear Post stood Nancy McClane watching the great Vs of geese going north overhead, watching the patterns the clouds made in the water and drinking of the crystal air.

Another winter had gone and though summer meant hard work, it was good to be alive just now. To be free and young and alive in the Far North. Work would begin within the week, but now there was rest and it was spring.

Nancy

Soon the planes would start winging south, winging north, sluggish in the air with cargoes of pitchblende and payrolls and machinery as the mining of radium went into full swing. And White Bear Landing was the halfway mark between the Arctic mines and civilization. Soon the lake would be struck and slashed by pontoon and slipstream and the thunder of mighty engines would become so monotonous that only its absence would be unusual.

Man was conquering the Arctic by air and White Bear Landing was only one of a hundred outposts, forgotten eight months of the year.

It was hard work but Nancy found a certain peace in it. This was her country and that of her father and now it was all she had—though she smiled to herself at the thought of possessing so vast a region.

Men grew harsh in their battle with snow and scowling forests, but few men had ever shown her discourtesy. If Taggart had not come down early that spring, she would never have had a passing doubt of her own safety here, though she was but a girl alone.

Taggart came. Three half-breeds in a long canoe, with Taggart hunched like the Russian Bear amidships, hungrily looking toward the landing and the post and store back of it. Log houses all, but they were something more than wilderness though something less than civilization.

Nancy did not know Taggart and she did not withdraw. She stood on the porch and watched the canoe ground in the sand.

Taggart got out. He was a tower of bone and sinew and his

checkered shirt was plastered tight to his muscular chest by sweat and spray. His beard had grown carelessly to mat over his coarse face and his eyes seemed to use the hair for cover.

Taggart had strength and he also had brains. But a lifetime of hard boom camps and the early discovery that brawn made law and brains made money had thrown Taggart into rough contact with the police too often for him not to have gained a reputation for badness.

He swaggered up the beach, looking at Nancy. He had not seen a woman for a year and a half, but even if this had not been the case, a sight of Nancy McClane made most men stop.

She was dressed in a calico shirt and a buckskin riding skirt and wore beaded moccasins made by the Crees. But she had been educated in a school most women name with awe and the stamp of it showed through this wilderness dress. There was a way her hair radiated the sunlight again, a way she looked and smiled and the proud carriage of her. She was beautiful even in the cities and in the north, men found it difficult to believe their eyes.

Taggart came to a stop below the porch. His coat was over his arm and a big Colt stuck out at an angle from his hip. Insolently he looked her up and down and then grinned happily.

Taggart

"Where's Durant?" said Taggart.

She was uneasy before this man as the slightest glance would have told anyone that here was a bully of the camps, a man without principle and ready to break the code. But she looked at him frankly. "He's gone up the lake to try the fishing. He'll be back in an hour."

"Yeah?" said Taggart. "I think you're lying. Never mind, shove a couple quarts out to these breeds and give me something good. No trade liquor for mine. I've got pound notes aplenty."

She went into the post, treading lightly over the bare boards and outwardly unconcerned. But she eyed the rifle rack with longing just the same.

She gave out the two quarts and then a bottle of Hudson's Bay Scotch to Taggart.

He was making a show for her benefit. He cracked off the top by hitting it against the fireplace and then drank around the jagged glass. He drank loudly and with great pleasure and when he was done the bottle was dry. He threw it into the fireplace.

"Gimme another," said Taggart. "I got pound notes enough to buy out the King, damn his soul. Huh, you ain't shocked! Must be a Yank."

She gave him another quart and took his pound notes and gave him change and then, very gently, she pointed to the sign above the blanket racks, "No drinking inside this post. Durant, Factor, White Bear Landing, Hudson's Bay Company."

Taggart chuckled and cracked the head off the bottle and drank again.

Slowly Nancy moved up the counter to the place Durant kept his Webley, watching Taggart the while. But the gun was not there and she suddenly remembered that Durant had taken it when he had left to bring in a trapper who had sent word for help. Durant would not be back for two days.

"Gimme another," said Taggart. "I'm dry. I ain't wet my whistle for a year and a half and I could hold a keg."

"Obviously," said Nancy, "but I don't think you had better try. Durant will be back any moment."

"Bah," said Taggart, "I got eyes. Your canoe house hasn't been opened since the ice broke. Look, I ain't a bad guy, sister . . ."

He edged slowly around the counter. "I'm tough but I ain't bad. I'm Taggart. Ask anybody and they'll tell you who Taggart is."

Nancy backed away. The gun racks were five paces to her right and she moved slowly in that direction.

Taggart took two quick steps and was between her and the guns. "Look, sweetheart, who's to know? I'm Taggart and I'm tough, but I ain't bad. You're the best lookin'—"

Suddenly she stopped and laughed at him. She tossed her brown hair back out of her eyes and her mirth was very real.

"That's better," said Taggart.

"Is it?" said Nancy. "Listen."

There was a far-off drumming which was growing gradually in the still air. Nancy laughed again. "That's a police plane, Mr. Taggart."

But Taggart was not worried, just then, about police. He had done nothing recently. But her laughter forced him back

7

and he took another fifth of Scotch from the rack and broke it on the counter and then leaned toward her across the boards, drinking.

"We'll see if the redcoat stops and if he don't, the party goes on."

She looked at him with contempt and walked toward the door. Taggart reached out and dragged her back.

"No signaling," said Taggart.

She shook herself free from him and went on.

The single-engined ship equipped with pontoons came streaking down the sky, banked steeply and, with cut gun and wires whining, sailed to a settling halt on the placid lake. With abrupt, important snorts, the plane taxied toward the shore to finally ground on the sand.

Two men in khaki tunics, wearing the insignia of the pilots of the Royal Mounted, got down and walked up toward the post, neither speaking, and both watching carefully before them.

One was a slender youngster with a very sensitive face which he made as hard as possible. The other was older, about twenty-nine, and he looked as though he had a ramrod for a backbone.

Nancy knew the youngster casually. He was Streak Faulkner, a rather reckless and thoughtless fellow. But the other she had never seen before. He looked strong and unswerving.

They came into the post with little ceremony. The older one said, "This Taggart, Streak?"

"Yeah," said Streak.

Streak

"Taggart, I'm Bob Dixon. Heard of me?"

Evidently Taggart had, as Nancy noticed him flinch. She looked with new respect at Constable Pilot Bob Dixon. Yes, there was steel in the man, and his face was as emotionless as though carved from iron. His gaze was level and penetrating. He had not glanced toward Nancy.

"We thought you'd be here," said Dixon. "Would you like to tell what you know about the Hanlon killing or shall I knock it out of you?"

"It's a lie," said Taggart, bristling and stalking forward. "It's a lie. I didn't have nothin' to do with Hanlon's shooting."

"I didn't say he was shot. And it happened night before last up at his placer." Dixon smiled without a hint of humor. "Keep on talking, Taggart. You'll hang sooner or later and this might as well be the time."

"Hang, will I?" said Taggart. "To hell with you, Mountie. I said I didn't know. . . ."

Dixon

Suddenly Bob Dixon's big fist balled up and crashed into Taggart's jaw. Taggart went down to his knees, shaking his head. Dixon yanked him to his feet and struck again but this time Taggart rushed. Dixon ducked and threw his weight sideways and sent the bigger man hurtling against the wall.

Deliberately, the Mountie advanced, jerked the man to his feet, plucked out the Colt and slammed Taggart down into a chair. Dixon did not appear to be ruffled. There was no anger in him, only thoroughness.

"Maybe he didn't do it," said Streak Faulkner, staring at Taggart's bloodied face.

"All rats are the same," snapped Dixon. "Even if he didn't, he's given more beatings than he's taken."

"Yeah," said Streak in a melancholy way, "but I think you go too far with this stuff sometimes, Bob."

Suddenly Nancy knew the Mountie. She had heard of him time after time. They called him "Lawbook" Dixon, but she had not known that he had been ordered to the Tokush River country.

Dixon slapped Taggart away with his gauntlets. Taggart lunged to get out of the chair but a hard blow smashed him back.

Nancy felt a little sick. She went out on the porch and looked at the lake but the day was no longer so crystal bright. In the room she heard an occasional blow and once a chair went over. And in a blood-chilling monotone, Dixon kept asking over and over about the killing. Taggart's voice was getting weak and once Streak interposed. He was a good kid, Streak. A little reckless and without too many brains, but men liked him.

At last they dragged Taggart out on the porch. The bully was a bully no more. His face was swollen and thick and his beard was dyed red in spots. Terror had its grip on him. His bedeviler had not even showed signs of weariness.

"If you didn't do it," said Dixon, relentlessly, "then how is it you have so many pound notes? Hanlon had a cache, they tell me, and it's empty. There were pound notes in that cache."

"I didn't get them from Hanlon!" cried Taggart, beaten down.

"Then where did they come from?" said Dixon.

"I'll tell you," whimpered Taggart. But he didn't. He sagged between them as though he was going to pass out.

Nancy watched because she couldn't look away. Taggart was tough and this was the first time Taggart had ever been whipped, that was plain. But he had been whipped and this chunk of granite in khaki, this Mountie without a heart, had done it without half trying. She did not recognize the cunning of intelligent training there.

They started to let Taggart down to the puncheon boards but he had only been shamming. With a wild back sweep of his arms, he sent both Mounties reeling and leaped off the porch to sprint for his canoe.

Dixon got up on one knee. "Stop, in the King's name!"

Taggart was too frightened to stop. He made the gunwale. The explosion of powder was like a physical blow to Nancy.

11

She saw Taggart stiffen, half in and half out of the craft. Gradually he sank sideways into the water and streamers of red fanned out from him.

Dixon walked down to him and pulled him to the shore. Taggart's hip was shattered by the big Webley slug and he slowly came around, moaning in pain.

"Damn you," whispered Taggart, "I was straight for once. Straight! The Crees been selling furs and I've been selling them bullets and traps and they had pound notes. I didn't know nothing about the Hanlon killing."

Streak patched him up with a first-aid kit and the two Mounties loaded him into the police ship.

"Take him down to Fort Ledeau," said Dixon. "I'll wait here."

"Okay," said Streak. "But I kinda wish you hadn't shot, Bob."

"All rats are the same," said Dixon.

Streak turned and taxied out into the lake and headed into the wind. He took off with a steep, climbing turn to give vent to his feelings.

Bob Dixon walked slowly back to the porch. "Sorry, Miss . . ."

"Nancy McClane."

He took off his helmet. "They're all the same, those fellows. They're yellow at heart and they terrorize every weaker person they meet. Say, that must have been nasty, having that fellow drunk on your hands. I'm glad we happened in."

"I was in no danger," said Nancy. "You are not the only one that knows tricks."

12

*She saw Taggart stiffen, half in and half out of the craft.
Gradually he sank sideways into the water and
streamers of red fanned out from him.*

He looked at her admiringly. "One wouldn't connect wrestling tricks with such a pretty girl—if you'll pardon me, Miss McClane. Say, you talk like a Yank."

"Yes."

"That's swell," said Dixon, but gravely. "My mother was a Yank. Are you up here with your father?"

"My father is dead."

"Oh. I'm sorry. Was he from this country?"

"From Virginia," said Nancy.

That struck a chord in Dixon. He frowned a little, searching his police file brain and then, eyes wide open in astonishment, he looked at Nancy and his calm was gone.

"Why . . . why that must have been Thomas McClane who was—" He stopped, embarrassed and now more than a little uneasy.

"Go ahead," said Nancy, coolly. "I see now why they call you 'Lawbook' Dixon. Go ahead. Certainly I'm the daughter of a criminal and criminals are all rats. Certainly. They arrested Thomas McClane for selling fraudulent stocks on a loaded mine and they put him in prison and he got tuberculosis and died. He was a gentleman, not a rat."

Uncomfortable, on more than one count, Dixon turned and went down to sit on the edge of the wharf and watch for Streak's return.

CHAPTER TWO

SUMMER had gone and the winter snows had blanketed the land. Ice in the rivers had broken at the first warm wind and now even the smallest creeks were great, foaming rivers as all the north country poured the dregs of an Arctic winter into the Arctic Sea.

At the police post, Fort Ledeau, Inspector Morency and Constable Pilot Streak Faulkner watched the sky, not for the great Vs which honked northward nor for the white and fleecy clouds, but for a single plane which was now a few minutes overdue.

Inspector Morency was a man grown gray in the service. He was not a severe fellow, as he had lived long and wisdom had come with years. He no longer thought himself spruce, as easy chairs had given him softness and a paunch and so his uniform was faded and unpressed. But his blue eyes were youthful and now showed some small worry.

Young Streak finally pointed, "There he comes."

"I'm getting old," said Morency with a sad smile. "Ears and eyes make no note of him, youngster." He shaded his face against the low lying sun in the south and at last picked up both hum and dot in the blue.

With deft hand and accurate eye, Bob Dixon brought the small plane curving in to a smooth landing on Lake Tiyo,

15

sending up great clouds of geese with his spray. He jabbed throttle and came on into the hangar ramp.

Streak raced ahead and arrived before Bob could get down on a pontoon and throw a line. Streak waded in and secured the ship.

"Hello, Streak," said Dixon with pleasure. "How's the north?"

"How's Montreal?" countered Streak.

"I haven't been there in a month. I've been over on the Tokush River. Had a vacation."

"Girl?" grinned Streak. "She's nice, I'll—"

"Girl?" said Dixon, puzzled. "Oh, you mean Thomas McClane's daughter. No, didn't even see her." He climbed up the sloping ramp and walked with Streak back toward Morency, who waited in the headquarters door. "Taggart went north when he left the hospital. Said he was out to get me and I thought I'd give him a chance."

"That was a bad play, Bob."

"They're all rats."

"Yes, but Taggart will never walk straight again."

"He never walked straight in the first place," said Dixon.

"Look, Bob, you know why you were called in here."

Morency

16

"No. Why?"

"Take it easy, that's all I can say now. As a friend, I advise you to quit sticking your chin out—"

"Hello, Dixon," said Morency, standing back so that they could enter the headquarters.

The place was bare to severity, the only spot of color the Union Jack on the wall, a flag given to Morency long years ago by the King for saving another flag in a forgotten war.

Morency was somber. He paced around to his chair and sat down. He picked up a pencil and made scrawls on a pad as though unwilling to begin.

Dixon saw that something was in the air and so he stood at attention before the desk, waiting.

Finally, Morency looked up. "Dixon, I received orders from Montreal to put you on a very strange case. I did not agree but I am not invited to give opinions."

He made some more scrawls and drew down his shaggy white brows. "You are not the man I would like to have. You did not know it but I sent you back to Montreal last year. Dixon, I have never approved of either your attitude or your methods. There are laws, certainly, but there is also such a thing as mercy."

Dixon stood seemingly unperturbed.

To reach the heart of the man, for all his wisdom, Morency thought he had to use stronger ammunition. "If you take this case I shall expect efficiency, yes. But also I want a little sense and less *law*. Am I clear?"

"I have always done my duty, sir," said Dixon, knowing it was trite, but knowing he had to say something.

"That Taggart blunder was bad, Dixon. Hanlon hired Crees to work his placer and paid them in pound notes and the Crees bought traps from Taggart. A Cree murdered Hanlon over a squaw. Oh, I know, you made the arrest. But Taggart went to the hospital and he was not guilty. True, he has been guilty of much that went unpunished . . ."

"Then I fail to see—" began Dixon.

"Yes," said Morency with a sigh, "you fail to see. Listen. A payroll plane has vanished. Don't look startled about not knowing, as the news has not been released. A payroll plane vanished, and Brandon of the Bear Tooth Mines has a theory of where it went. A young fellow named Gregory hasn't been heard from since he left White Bear Landing. . . . Oh, I know he might have been forced down, but Brandon has another idea. Brandon says it was robbery, and he has his reasons, which he says he will divulge when he has more proof. You are to take Brandon with you and search the waterways north of White Bear Landing, all the way to the headwaters of the Tokush River."

"Am I to leave now?" said Dixon.

"Wait. Dixon, I wish they didn't think so well of you in Montreal. I think it has gone to your head. No offense; I am telling you for your own good. Your father was once the greatest judge in the Dominion, and that gives you a boost. But your head is full of law, Dixon. God knows why you never became a lawyer, as your father wished. You have a lot to learn. And if you tag any suspects on this case, I shall expect you to forget law and use common sense. Am I understood?"

Dixon's face was white and his hands were trembling. He was looking over Morency's head. "Yessir."

"We cut short your vacation, I believe," said Morency. "Solve this case with mercy and common sense and I'll do something handsome for you. I'll recommend—"

"Thank you," said Dixon, tight-lipped and stiff.

"Very well, then," said Morency. "Brandon is waiting, and you can leave immediately for White Bear Landing."

Dixon stalked out. His eyes were hard and bleak and his fists were clenched and Streak, pacing beside him, said, "Take it easy. He's trying to do you a favor, Bob. He likes you. Honest, he does. He says you'll head the Royal Mounted someday, and he wants you to head it well."

"He can save his likes," said Dixon, bitterly.

They reached the plane in silence and Dixon threw down his dunnage sack. He had recovered himself a little. "Toss it in the hangar, will you, Streak? I'll pick it up when I come back."

"Sure," said Streak. "You're pretty tough, Bob."

"Yeah," said Dixon. "I'm pretty tough."

Brandon came out of the post store and walked across to them. He was a serious fellow, more interested in his business and money than he was in the fate of Gregory, his pilot. He was dressed all out of place for the north, wearing a neat black suit and a snap-brim hat.

"You Dixon?" he said, extending his hand.

Dixon took it doubtfully. "Yes."

"Glad to meet you, Dixon. I think I'm lucky. A man with

your rep can do a lot for this country. They tell me you're the toughest Mountie in Canada, and I guess a man would have to be pretty damned brave to do the things you've done. Law and law to the letter, that's what we need, Dixon, and you're the man—"

"Will you get in?" said Dixon, sickened by the flattery.

Brandon got into the front cockpit and Dixon stood for a moment on the pontoon, buckling his helmet. The plane had been gassed in his absence and a mechanic was starting the engine.

"Take it easy, Bob," said Streak.

"Sure," said Dixon. "Sure, I'll take it easy. See you in a couple days. I think I'll want to get drunk."

"Don't start that again, Bob."

"More advice? Haven't I always reported sober?"

"Well . . . yes."

"Let a guy alone, will you?"

The tone hurt Streak but he guessed he had deserved it. He didn't look up again. He shoved the ship out into the lake with a hard push and gave Dixon a salute which was not answered. Streak walked disconsolately up the runway to carry the bag into the hangar.

It was spring, but all freshness was gone for Dixon. He gunned savagely through swimming geese and rocketed his ship skyward with a jerk, which he knew with vicious joy had turned Brandon's stomach wrong side out.

He swung brutally about into the course for White Bear Landing and the shadow of the plane whipped the rolling forests and streams below and the engine's roar sent the echoes into raucous life.

Dixon's eyes were bleak and he felt much wronged—and much reason he had.

His father! His father, the greatest judge in the Dominion! And "Lawbook" Dixon, how he hated that name!

He hated the world in that hour, hated it for the things it had done to a boy who had tried to play by the rules, who had tried to find affection, always denied, who had tried to be kind and cheerful and who had received for his efforts backslaps at every hand.

"Lawbook" Dixon. And why not? He had taken in statutes as vitamins in his milk. He had stumbled through a household as a child, a household run like a court, with the great judge always on the bench and sentence forever being meted.

Late for school. Three days in his room. Late for lunch, and no lunch was his. Shoes wet from wading, and his allowance was gone.

Year in and year out, discipline harsh and unyielding, because the great judge said that this was the only way to make a man. Either make him or break him. And Bob Dixon had yet to be broken.

"Lawbook" Dixon! How he hated that name. How he hated the law itself and every letter in every one of its sections and paragraphs. Tomes without number they had poured into his head and then, when he had suddenly stepped forth one night and had gotten drunk enough to forget, the great judge had sat upon his bench in the house and had told him that he was disappointed in a son who had always been wayward, that the goal of such a one was the cells, that life had a way of treating men who sinned.

The great judge on the bench, ruling the life of an intelligent boy for twenty-four endless years. The law, the law, the law. And if you did not know the law, then the law would break you and kill you.

Respect the law, stand in terror of the law, and at last the law would come stalking after you.

And the great judge on the bench had been disappointed in a son who had gotten drunk but once and had taken him from school and had cast him out.

There were two courses open. But Bob Dixon feared the law and the only safety for him lay within the law. And now he had fought his way up to be a Constable Pilot, but at any moment that great vulture, LAW, was liable to crash its gavel into his skull. One slip on duty and he was done.

He was convinced of it. He could never forget it. And convinced was he, also, that all criminals were rats. A man cannot be taught a thing for twenty-four bitter years without carrying that thing with him the rest of his life.

Yes, he had wanted to show the great judge, that martinet of a father, that he knew the law, and that was part of it too. But more than that was hatred as burning as acid in his brain for those things which had made his life an endless nightmare. Yes, he was running away. He was taking the best protection against the law by being the law itself.

And all criminals were rats.

That beautiful girl at White Bear Landing . . . He had

wanted to see more of her, but he did not dare. Her father had died in a prison, and perhaps, if he saw that girl, no matter how much he liked to be with her, she would soften him and make him a victim of this law he carried like a torch, but knowing always that it would eventually sear him.

The plane gunned over the flowing forest land, throwing its shadow down as a challenge to the gloom of the timber, to the wolves in their lairs and the stalking panther on the bough. Challenging the criminal, challenging the world.

Mercy. What did any man know of mercy? He had never been shown mercy. Why did he have to be as he was, hated and feared throughout the North?

But criminals were rats. He must never forget that, lest someday he fall and the law take him.

They swerved over the lake at White Bear Landing and lanced northward, above the rolling forest land, with the Tokush brawling as it poured trees and broken ice toward the Arctic Sea. He ruddered again to sweep out and west to intercept the headwaters of the river, and two shadows began to race where only one had been before.

At long last, Bob Dixon became conscious of the other engine, above and behind. He turned to look, shielding his goggled eyes. Brandon also turned to stare.

The plane was not a police ship. Dixon had no way of recognizing it. But Brandon had. It was his own fast biplane, the very ship for which they searched!

Dixon understood the danger from Brandon's suddenly contracted face. Again he looked back and up, peering closely.

The plane was faster than his, but it was following almost casually. Maybe Gregory had repaired his engine and now wanted protection. . . .

But that was not true!

Abruptly the black payroll plane went over the hump and started a dive. Dixon kicked his throttle with the heel of his hand, but the police ship had little speed left.

Wide open, the black ship was diving and the prop was growing bigger and brighter. Suddenly red pom-poms began to cut through it, and fabric lashed up all along the police ship's fuselage.

Dixon verticaled. The other ship flashed past and looped up to fire another burst.

Machine guns! And the police ship was unarmed.

Dixon curved away, wide open, and heaven and earth scrambled in a hotchpotch of speed.

But this plane was no match for the other, and Dixon, looking back, knew that he was done.

Brandon's mouth was leaking scarlet and he was slumped in a posture which could mean only death, his head lolling back and forth as the ship lunged.

With a scream the engine revved up and Dixon swiftly pulled throttle. His prop was gone, in silver fragments, out into the sky. Below was a wide place in the Tokush and with luck he could make it.

But luck was not given to him. Smoke lashed back at him in tongues of hot flame.

Bullets spattered all about him.

He whipped open his belt and took one last look at the dead mine chief, and then sprang upward into his slipstream to spin through the empty air.

He waited until the last two hundred feet to pull his rip cord and then the chute cracked open.

The black ship was circling as he settled, but it did not fire again.

And Dixon could not understand why. He was an easy target in those few seconds.

He slipped his chute to let him down in a small clearing, and then, digging in his heels to stop the full silk from dragging him, he spilled its wind and flung off the harness to dive into the cover of a tree.

A loud detonation nearer the river marked the end of his plane. The black ship was coming down in spirals. Smoke was billowing in a great cloud above the trees.

Dixon started forward, but the black ship did not land. It turned at last and vanished into the north.

Limping and sorely puzzled, Dixon started down the river bank toward White Bear Landing.

*He whipped open his belt and took one last look at the
dead mine chief, and then sprang upward into his slipstream
to spin through the empty air.*

CHAPTER THREE

IT was morning but Bob Dixon was too weary to move and lay looking up at the ceiling of the barracks, thinking how nice it was just to stay still and not have to get up and drag a few more miles.

The flight he had made in three and a half hours from Ledeau had been far enough to make three weeks of walking. He had failed to sight a single trapper as he had swung out from the river to try to make the high ground and better time. He had used up his cartridges on game. He had lost his way and found it again. He had been without fire or cover or food for days together. . . .

But he was back and the nightmare march was over and for three days now he had lain here getting back his strength. This morning he would get up, but just now he was completely at peace, even the memory of his crash wiped out by even harder fates, and those in turn had become a long montage which was now almost forgotten in itself.

He was at rest and it was good. Lying here this way, not having to keep up his guard, not having to play a part, with nothing to bother him but the lazy buzzing of a fly at the window. Yes, it was good.

And decent it had been of everyone to leave him completely

alone. That had been the most thoughtful thing possible and he hadn't known that any of them except Streak had liked him that much.

Finally he got up and stretched. He bathed and shaved and dressed in clean, cool khaki and looked at himself in the steel mirror above the wash bench. Funny how hard he had worked to keep up that front. And now it was almost automatic, as though he lived inside another person, and the other person could not be touched.

He strolled out across the compound, feeling like a gentlemen of leisure, and stepped into the cook shack.

The cook was there, but he looked up only once and after that he did not speak. The fellow had never been surly before. On the contrary, this French-Canadian had been groveling before him, much to Dixon's disgust.

But now the fellow spoke not at all and merely dumped some cold food into a pannikin and sent it carelessly sliding down the table to Dixon, with the knife and fork jangling after.

And still he did not speak. He went outside and sat down and smoked a cigarette, as though waiting patiently for Dixon to be gone.

Troubled a little, Bob nibbled at the food. His worry increased and suddenly he stood up and pushed the dish away. He looked first at the cook and then at the headquarters, above which the jack floated in the morning wind.

But there was no cause for this, he was sure. The cook was having an off day, that was all.

He went outside and lighted a cigarette himself, strolling as though nothing in the world troubled him.

Two constables stopped talking as he came up and looked the other way. In surprise, he stared at them. But he shrugged and turned back. Slowly he paced down to the gate, where the man on duty was usually ready for a chin-chin. But now the sentry stood very erect and saw nothing and said nothing.

Bob looked him up and down and then, in abrupt wonder, whirled to face headquarters. Streak was running toward him, glancing to the right and left, as he came, at other men who had appeared to silently stand looking away from Dixon.

"Go see Morency," said Streak, looking frightened.

"What's this all about?" demanded Bob.

"Can't talk to you. Sorry, orders. Go see Morency."

Certain that some awful mistake had been made, Bob sped with swift stride to headquarters.

Morency heard him coming and looked at his blotter. He dug a nail under the side of his pencil and lifted a sliver out.

"You wanted to see me, sir?" said Dixon.

Morency could not look up. He made stars on a scratch pad. "I probably caused this, Dixon. You were mad at me and so you did it. Or maybe you did it before. I—"

"What are you talking about?" snapped Dixon, in an unmilitary manner. Suddenly he felt the walls closing in on him, and out at the gate the sentry was blocking the way. Something terrible had gone wrong with the LAW.

He could hear the great judge saying in his nasal voice, "You are wayward, Robert. Some day you will run afoul of the law and become a disgrace to us all. Some day they will imprison you. . . ."

Was that ghastly nightmare of prophecy coming true?

29

Two constables had moved into the room from another door. They were armed, and between them they had a half-breed of unsavory appearance.

Morency looked up and he appeared as a man who has been deeply wounded. "We know, you see."

Dixon stared around him. The constables were looking straight ahead. They had once been his friends. . . .

"Know what?" said Bob in a voice much too loud.

"About your crash, about your vacation. Everything, Dixon. Simmons, let the half-breed talk."

The half-breed was suspiciously willing and surprisingly logical. "Me see'm, almost one mont' ago, by gar. H' I'm down in de woods and I see'm. Police plane, she come over, so! Come down to land—so! In Tokush River. H' I'm scared, don't know why. She come down, and this redcoat, he get hout and then, *mon Dieu,* she grab little feller and choke'm and shoot'm—boom-boom—*so!* By gar, H' I'm run right away for de canoe and come on to Fort Ledeau. H' I'm scared. H' I'm see'm this feller, she go way up and fly away, so!"

"It's a lie!" shouted Dixon. "It's a damned lie! This man is not telling the truth. I reported what happened!"

"Then what became of the plane?" said Morency slowly. Dixon stared at him.

"And how is it that we found most of the missing payroll in your dunnage bag when we looked, after this half-breed told his story."

"You're framing me!" shouted Dixon. "Goddamn you, you can't do this to me! There's my record, there's—"

"Aye, your record," said Morency. "You've been a merciless

man, Dixon, and, as in the Taggart case, you showed brutality beyond any—"

"Damn you!" cried Dixon, striving to reach the inspector.

The two constables had him and no Mountie tricks could be played on two strong Mounties, fight though Dixon did. The half-breed stood back, smiling. And then, unnoticed, he drifted quietly out of the door and so out of the fort.

"Steady," said Morency. "All this wild display is guilt enough in itself. You're caught, and caught fairly. But the evidence is slim. Indeed, it might very well be framed. There is not enough here for a case, there is only suspicion. I would never risk such flimsy stuff in court."

He stopped and looked at the disheveled Dixon who still tried insanely to break the grips his fellows had upon him.

"Steady," said Morency in a sharp voice.

Dixon stopped and stared at him, and hardly saw him at all.

"There is no reason to drag the name of the Royal Mounted through the courts," said Morency. "You never showed anyone mercy and now you really should be entitled to none. But I know that conviction is impossible and I know too well the fate to which you will be thrown, once out of a red coat. This entire north country will turn on you, Dixon. Here, I have written your resignation. Sign it."

They released him. He was quieter now but there was a strange light of disbelief in his eyes. Blankly he looked at the resignation and then, abruptly, he knew what had happened to him.

And still, he did not break. He squared his shoulders and gave his tunic a tug, and looked very cool.

31

"In the courts I would have no chance—and you know it, Morency. But I have even less chance out there." He flung his hand toward the timber. "What I have done I have had to do, but you would not understand. Yes, I'll resign and thank you for the chance of getting the man who must have done this to me."

"Bravado," said Morency. "But if it makes you feel better, go ahead. You'll drink up your pay and we'll find you in a gutter of a boom town with a slug in your back. The Royal Mounted has not liked you, Dixon, and neither has the North. Such tactics we knew were used to cover something else. You haven't a human emotion in you, and not one of us will weep when you are gone. Sign, and get out of this post!"

Morency saw a certain mercy in his own deed. He was giving the man a chance, lashing him on, so that Dixon would try to prove him wrong.

"Yes," said Dixon. "Yes. That's right. Not a human . . ."

He looked as though he would fall, but he clutched the desk. Somehow he found the pen and scrawled his name across the sheet.

He faced about and stumbled through the sunshine to the barracks. He took his own rifle and Webley and changed to woods boots and clothes and then, with slim pack, and all else left behind him, he made his way down to the water's edge and, with difficulty, pulled his own canoe from the shed and launched it.

He did not look back. His paddle strokes were slow.

CHAPTER FOUR

SUMMER blossomed from spring and all the north country was in a fever of activity, to make the most of the short months of warmth.

At White Bear Landing planes, making their first stop inside the Arctic Circle, were swift to take off again for the scattered mining towns. Machinery could be flown swiftly in, but the loads had to be small, and the pitchblende coming out was the accumulation of the work in the winter past, as well as tripled production through the warm months.

All was activity at White Bear Landing. All was haste and bustle. Camps sprung up and fell back overnight, leaving not so much as a curl of woodsmoke to mark the arrival and departure of men.

Summer, and the Arctic was on the move.

But one man, in the chilly wind of night, sat alone before the scattered embers of his fire and did not move.

He had tried and he had failed, and now he was close to the cracking point, naked to every revengeful wind that blew, to all the eyes which stared and the lips which curled in contempt.

He had tried. He had worn his flesh from his fingers driving his canoe from river to river in his search of Taggart. But the man had been swallowed in the illimitable forests of darkness, in the mountains and glaciers and unmapped lakes just south of the Pole.

He had tried another way. He had offered his services in return for the use of a plane. He had wanted to search from the air. But mining officials had laughed at him, pointing out, in all truth, that he had no civilian pilot's license.

The whole North knew. Not the details, which made it worse. Men at lonely fires make talk grow. And so no one knew and believed the worst.

And deep in the forest of White Bear, Bob Dixon looked at the dying coals and found no answer there or anywhere. They were still afraid of his strength, but that he did not know. He had been safe within the law, but now he was no longer safe from law.

For twenty-four years he had been whipped with the threats of awful justice. That he could never forget. No amount of personal courage, no amount of striving, no amount of glory gained could ever make him forget.

A great judge, hunch-shouldered on his bench, had ruled his home as well. But no jury was in that home, no mercy tempered law.

And now until his dying day, so long as he stayed in contact with the world of men, Bob Dixon would envision the LAW as a great bird of prey with ready, outstretched talons.

Twenty-four years, and no amount of deeds could ever undo or disprove that teaching.

The words of that prophecy rang in his ears as loudly as they had been uttered five years before.

Suddenly he moved. He reached into his open pack and

pulled forth a bottle of rum. He could not stand it any more. He could not sit here with his thoughts howling at him.

Dead in a gutter, with a bullet in his back. Yes, and he prayed to God it would be soon.

He drank deeply and put the bottle down. The rum scalded his throat but that was all. He tried again without success. He waited and the thoughts dinned on.

Darker and darker grew the fire. Lower and lower sank the level of the bottle.

And still he could not forget.

Dead in the gutter, with a bullet in his back. Yes. He had been a fool. He was the only one to blame. He had been a fool, mad with the power of a uniform . . . but no. Even that uniform had made him uneasy. Even the presence of Mounties had often made him restless and had as often made him snap curt answers at his fellows.

But he had been a fool.

He drank more deeply than ever.

Taggart was out there, laughing at him. Taggart was waiting and watching for him to crack. Let him watch. Let him. All too soon . . . but not soon enough.

The butt of his Webley was at his side, hard against him. He took another drink and then set the bottle down, looking at it in the slowly lessening light. It had no effect. His thoughts went on and would not stop. He was going mad, he knew. And all the thickening darkness was alive with eyes, watching him, ready to rush against him and strike him down should they see the way clear.

Well, he would clear the way. And he even laughed a little.

He had been brave long enough. He had dared walk where others dared not step. He had challenged the world and the world had stood back.

Yes, he had done that. "Lawbook" Dixon. That was funny when one remembered how he had hated LAW. The world was blind and could not read.

And now the world was waiting and the night was a curtain of velvet. One last ember pulsating in dead ashes was all the light he had now.

And in a moment it would be gone.

He took out the Webley and turned it in his hand. He knew what it could do, and now the time had come for its last shot.

The ember was almost out and he smiled a bit as he saw it go. He turned the muzzle of the gun to his face and thrust the hard front sight back of his teeth. His finger began to tighten.

Suddenly the gun roared but the bullet had only seared his cheek and the noise had hurt his ear.

Stunned and leaping back, striving to make out what had struck at him, he saw a vague figure moving before him.

Wood cracked as it was broken and laid upon the ashes. Tiny flames began to creep up, and the light reached out and Dixon saw the girl.

She looked angry and it made her more beautiful than ever. Her hair had been whipped by the evening wind and hung down to her shoulders in even, natural waves. Her sensitive face, though half in shadow, did not well hide the emotional strain within her. She was dressed in a beaded buckskin jacket and skirt and mosquito boots, and even at this moment part of Dixon remarked that oddity of girl and dress. In clothing she was an Indian. In breeding she was a white princess. A far cry from Vassar to the north country and buckskin.

He felt guilty then. He slid the Webley back into its holster as he stood up.

"Why did you come?"

"You've been a fool long enough, Bob Dixon."

"I don't have to be told."

"For more than a month I have watched you come and go, watched you walk like an old man, when you are so young! And when you did not come into the landing today, I hurried to finish my work to find out why."

"There's no reason for you to be concerned."

She looked at him for almost a minute without speaking. And then, "So it was just front, after all."

That was dangerous to say, and he flared. "If you believe these yapping—"

"Hush. I meant your red coat. It was your front, your armor and how hard you worked to keep it, how many things you did to make certain you would never lose it. . . . Oh, I've watched you, Bob Dixon. The last weeks I have begun to understand as fragments about you came to me. At first I thought—but that is unimportant."

He sank down on his heels, and the fire began to play more brightly through the camp. "Why this concern for me?"

"Maybe any woman is concerned when she sees a man

dying before her eyes and thinks she can help him. But pull
your chin up and smile a little. Old boy, if I had had another
dish to wash, that dish would have sent you whither bound."

She was making it easy for him and he appreciated it.
Neither of them felt like levity and yet levity can sometimes
serve.

The fire was crackling in a lively way and he could see her
more clearly as she sat down upon a log close by him. She
warmed her hands, respecting his silence, and looked into
the flames.

He saw those hands. They were long-fingered and delicately
made, and they had expressive grace. But the skin was chafed
and reddened, and abruptly he recalled her last remark.

"Dishes? Certainly you don't wash dishes!"

"Why not?" she shrugged.

"But . . . but I thought this . . . I thought you merely waited
on the trading post customers."

"And cooked the meals and washed the plates and scrubbed
the floors and counted inventory and served drinks. . . . Ah,
let's not talk about it, Bob."

He was stirred to resentment by such circumstance. "But
that's not right! You . . . you've got a fine education, and your
people . . ."

"I have no people—now."

"I'm sorry. I forget. . . ."

"Sorry for what?" said Nancy. "Sorry to speak truth?
Oh yes, Bob Dixon, I can understand and, understanding,
know you."

"What do you mean?"

"A great judge in Montreal sent Thomas McClane to prison for fraud. And he gave a gentleman a lecture on morals, along with the sentence. And that judge is named Dixon."

He stared at her, incredulous.

"Oh, there's nothing so strange about it," said Nancy, with another small shrug. "The People versus Thomas McClane was a big case, and included big people. There was nothing small and nothing mean about it. Bankers dropped a million and a half and began to howl for blood, and courts lean on the side of the most expensive lawyer. A big case, a great judge . . ."

"Then you've seen Judge Dixon?"

"On the bench," said Nancy. "On the bench, surrounded by all the redcoats and the clerks and vassals and bootlicks. On the bench in a great black gown with vulture's wings for sleeves. And I heard his lecture on morals."

She laughed a little and he wished she hadn't, the sound was such a bitter one.

She went on in a moment. "And so I know you, Bob Dixon, and I think you know me . . ."

"But I don't know so much," he begged.

"What is there to tell? I get forty in summer and twenty in winter, and my food and bed. And old Durant is parsimonious, but otherwise as right as an ancient Scot can be. And the Crees like me and I speak their tongue, and most of the men respect me to a point of ridiculousness—and thrash those others who won't."

"But you can't go on like that forever," said Bob.

"No. No, I can't go on like that forever. And sometimes I am so tired, I think . . . No. You have enough woes. But did you ever feel that you were a weathercock to be buffeted by every wind that blows, that there is no faith left in life and nothing matters. . . . No. I'll cheer up. . . . That's funny. I come out to cheer you and then I feel like crying. I guess . . . I guess I'm not much, after all."

"You are!" cried Bob with startling vehemence. He jumped up and kicked the fire together and the flames leaped up toward the overhanging green boughs, and the light reached down the narrow aisles between the trees.

He faced her and then sat down beside her and took her hands in his roughened own.

"Look . . . I . . . I don't know how to say it . . ."

She stopped him. "You poor kid, your hands are shaking like leaves."

"I'm scared."

"Bob Dixon scared?" she smiled. "The great Dixon? How the world would gape at that. But we won't tell, will we?"

"No. No, that's it. You know and I know. I'm scared and you're scared but nobody else knows. Look. Look. I want to help . . ."

"Yes. I know. But don't forget," said Nancy, "that you are the one that really needs the help. You're the most dangerous man in the north country and men jump a foot when you so much as light a match. But you've forgotten. You don't need a red coat. And today I told myself that if you didn't come, and if you were all right, I would give you something."

"You've already given me my life."

"Listen, Bob, the Big Chief Mine has not been visited for three years. The bankers have forgotten it. Machinery was flown in to the lake and the cabins are still intact and stocked because it was more expensive to fly the goods out than to write them off. There's everything there, and game in the hills about."

"Where is it?"

"You know the Tatnoosh Range? And Miller's Peak? Twenty miles southwest of Miller's Peak is a lake. You've never heard of it? Well, it's there. A fairly big lake, lying in the bottom of a crater some fifteen miles across at the top. There's everything in that basin in the way of game. There's everything at the Big Chief Mine, even unto guns and can openers. Oh, yes, it's all abandoned, but no one has been there. How do I know? Because it is only possible to fly in. No wall around the peak could be scaled, except by the greatest of mountaineers. But with a plane, it is simple as there is the lake. That was why Dad opened up that mine. He believed . . . but no matter. It is a beautiful spot and no one can reach it except from the air—"

"But wait. I have no plane. I have no money to hire a plane, and doubt if anyone would . . ."

"That is your problem."

"Yes," he said, rebuked.

"And Taggart is still your problem."

"Yes . . . Taggart."

"And there is still law and that must be appeased."

"I know," he said wearily.

She got up and again kicked the fire together and the flames crackled and danced.

41

Suddenly they looked at each other and smiled. And from a smile they laughed.

"It's good," said Nancy.

"What?"

"Life. Suddenly it's terribly good to live!"

CHAPTER FIVE

THE following night at Fort Ledeau, Streak Faulkner sat in gloomy silence on the edge of the ramp before the deserted hangar. The waves lap-lap-lapped mournfully against the moss-grown logs, and the wind sighed and whimpered in the spruce along the velvet-curtained shore.

An arctic owl chuckled as it soared down the lake on motionless and silent wings. It swerved inland and there was a small and forlorn squeak. Wings fanned for an instant and then the great owl whispered back along its course, dead rabbit dangling limply from its talons.

Streak shivered and did not know why. Ever since Bob Dixon had gone on that fateful trip with Brandon, Streak had felt alone. He thought it was because he had once been Dixon's friend, because he had not been able to help, because he had been so curt that last, terrible day. But these were not the causes. He had lost a friend. He had lost the comradeship and the protection of the strongest and hardest man in the Royal Mounted.

He could never believe there was any truth in what had happened. He could more than guess that Taggart loomed large in the affair. But Streak had the misfortune to be Bob Dixon's only close friend. And no matter what the others thought, Streak Faulkner had listened to Dixon across lonely fires in far camp, and he could vaguely guess with reason and could feel with strength that Bob Dixon was two men.

Almost at his elbow, startling him half out of his wits, an orderly loomed and spoke. "Something doing, Streak. Morency's got to see you right away."

"About . . . ?"

"Yes. Morency's out of his mind!"

Streak went at a run across the sandy beach and into the post. The door to headquarters was wide open and nervous boot beats sounded on the bare floor.

Morency was walking like a caged animal, fists clenched and jaw grim.

"You wanted me, sir?" said Streak.

Morency looked at him without seeing him and then whirled about and sank down in his chair.

"Some news, sir?"

"Hello. Yes. Yes, some news." Morency pulled himself together and straightened his tunic. "I'm in for it, Faulkner."

"I'm sorry to hear that, sir. If I can—"

"Yes, you can. Listen, Faulkner, Judge Dixon somehow got wind of what lay behind his boy's resignation. Dixon has power in Montreal."

"You mean he's after your hide . . . I mean, because you . . ."

"Yes," said Morency. "I can't understand it, Streak. Honest-to-God, I can't understand it!" He forgot the difference in position, discipline and form, and looked at Streak like a man who very badly wants an answer. "He must be made out of granite! He can't have any heart! Streak, he's asking for my resignation because I failed to bring the case to trial—because I failed to drag his boy through the muck of courts and papers. He . . . he says in this letter, which was forwarded to me, that he will not have Robert Dixon made an exception to the law just because he is the son of a Montreal judge. He says we cannot weaken our laws by making such exceptions. He . . . damn it, Streak! He's not human!"

"What are you going to do?" said Streak, scared at the guess which flashed into his mind.

Morency looked like a whipped dog. His voice was very low. "What can I do, Streak? I can't resign. I've got a wife. I've got a boy in Oxford. I won't be eligible for retired pay. . . ."

Streak knew then why he had been called. For once in his hard-riding life, Morency could not face a decision.

"If we bring it to trial," said Streak, "there's some small chance—"

"Not with Judge Dixon on the bench. And he will be! The fool thinks his own honor is at stake when his boy—"

"You want me to say it," said Streak. "You want me to volunteer to go out and get Bob Dixon and fly him to Montreal for the trial. You're afraid nobody but me could get him without his fighting back and escaping."

"Don't put it that way, Streak."

Streak was young and his decision was made. He reached across the desk for a sheet of paper and a pen.

"What are you going to do?" said Morency.

"If I remember rightly, the resignation form runs—"

"Faulkner!"

45

"Yes. Constable Faulkner, about to become Mr. Faulkner, a pilot out of a job."

"But . . ."

Streak wrote steadily on.

Footsteps sounded in the compound and, a moment later, a coatless operator from the radio room rushed in the door, a sheet in his hand.

Morency hardly saw the man but he took the slip, still looking at Streak's moving pen. And then he read the message. Suddenly he reached across the table and put his hand on the bottom of the page so that Streak could not go on.

Morency was himself again, hard-eyed and efficient. "Faulkner, something has happened. He either got wind of this or something is up."

Streak watched the paper in Morency's hand as the inspector read.

"White Bear Landing to Inspector Morency, Fort Ledeau. Report theft of payroll plane at dawn this morning. Flew out to search but must report failure to locate. Dixon missing since last night, his camp empty. Payroll plane was Lucky Horseshoe Radium Mine, money-bags ashore and safe. Constable Pilot Henderson."

Streak was as one struck by a bullet. He wanted to protest, he wanted to rip that message in strips. But he stood there woodenly.

"The Lucky Horseshoe Mine ships were all armed after that robbery," said Morency. "It carries a Vickers bow machine gun and can make two hundred and five at cruising. I am going to borrow a Snipe Fighter from the army, and it will be here tomorrow. If Henderson or Gates or Thompson take that ship and meet . . ."

Streak balled up his resignation. "Meet Dixon and shoot him down without a chance. You said yourself he wouldn't kill me—and he might hold his fire. There's just enough of a chance . . . I'm taking that Snipe Fighter, inspector. You brought me in here to ask me to bring Dixon back. I'll bring him back and show the whole lot of you that he's square."

Morency nodded. "Only one thing, Faulkner. You have the advantage of him. Unless you press that advantage, you will never succeed. My advice . . . But go do it your own way. He can't be square now, and things are going to happen and happen fast!"

CHAPTER SIX

O N a lake forgotten amid a thousand unmapped lakes, deep in a dark forest which gloomily overhung the banks, a campfire built of dry and smokeless wood crackled in the morning air. Close at hand was a green silk tent and nearby, at the water's edge, was a hangar built of interlocked boughs where a black seaplane crouched motionless.

Taggart sat with his leg extended before him and watched Gregory fry salt meat. Taggart had undergone a change. His face was thinner, and he had shaved his beard. His ugly, thin mouth had a cynical droop and the madness of anger was never quite gone from his eyes. He would never walk again without the aid of a cane, but during his year in the south he had had much time to make up for his lost physical strength by carefully sifting plans.

Gregory was a tall and surly fellow, not very intelligent and bearing a grudge against all the world. He had but one asset and that was excellent piloting skill. The war had twisted Gregory's belief in right and wrong, and he saw no good in anything. He had his medals for fifteen enemy planes, but for five years following the war he had almost starved—and that had been his climax. First doubt of the world's sanity and then conviction that the world was an evil place and all men were to be distrusted. He had asked for a raise in pay and Brandon, now amply repaid, had threatened to fire him. He had been ripe for Taggart's scheme, and now Taggart had him by holding the club of exposure over him.

A rhythmic dipping sound came faintly to Taggart and he struggled to sit erect, propping himself up by gripping his cane. Finally he saw the canoe, racing close under the shore and heading straight for the camp.

"It's LeCroix!" said Gregory.

"About time," said Taggart.

"Yeah, and if he ain't got good news, I'll wring his neck. Damn sitting here doing nothing. Almost two months now and that fool Dixon sticks around White Bear Landing. . . ."

"Maybe he's made a break," said Taggart, licking his lips.

LeCroix, the half-breed who had confronted Morency with his lying tale, beached his canoe and leaped out, giving the gunwale a tug to ground the keel. He came grinning up to the fire and looked from Taggart to Gregory.

"Spill it!" said Taggart irritably. "Damn you, you've waited long enough!"

"Three days ago, H' I'm leave White Bear, paddle like hell. By gar, she's done it. Dixon, she's steal a Lucky Horseshoe plane and go like hell-damn."

Taggart pried himself erect. Gregory let the salt meat burn and dashed into the tent for his helmet.

"Wait," said LeCroix, grinning. "H' I'm get this news plenty fast and H' I'm tell redcoats plenty big lie. H' I'm tell you a big payroll she's going through White Bear all de time. H' I'm fixum this Dixon and she's finish! Now me, H' I'm want one third the cash. H' I'm no damn voyageur, H' I'm plenty smart feller, by gar. H' I'm get one third cash or takum truth to redcoats."

Taggart looked at him for a long time, his eyes very bleak. "Okay, LeCroix, that's all right with me. Now go down there and start taking those boughs away from the ship while we get set."

"Hokay!" cried LeCroix happily. "H' I'm buy plenty present for de old squaw now. She say H' I'm plenty dumb but I tellum different now, by gar. H' I'm a rich man!"

He did a pivoting dance step and then began to sing as he waltzed down to the beach. He was a silly, empty-headed voyageur and nothing more.

He started to take the boughs away from the front of the makeshift hangar, balancing himself, as only a French boatman can, on the two logs which make the breakwater.

Taggart drew his Colt and cocked it. He raised the muzzle level with his belt and squeezed the trigger.

The explosion drew Gregory out of the tent. He stopped and stared blankly at the water.

LeCroix was sinking out of sight and only one hand moved feebly. Then he was gone, and a few red-frothed bubbles broke the quiet surface of the lake.

"Get moving," said Taggart. "We'll wait on the Tokush, at Caribou Bend, and nail that Lucky Horseshoe plane."

"But if—"

"To hell with 'If'! Dixon's taken it on the wing, and we've got him where we want him. We get the cash and he gets the chair. Use your brains if you've got any. Now warm up that engine, while I check these bullet drums."

CHAPTER SEVEN

L EONARD, pilot for the Lucky Horseshoe Mine, never had a chance. No combat training had been his and so he made the mistake of looking on his own level as he winged across the rolling forests.

And up in the sun, the champion of half a hundred dogfights looked without an emotion, unless it was one of greed, down upon the silver ship which sped with frantic haste into the north. He recognized Leonard by his flying habits, and knew that he had to deal with a raw kid recently out of flying school. Leonard had never been friendly to Gregory, because he was not attracted by sour mien and remark, and so it was with little remorse that Gregory eased his stick ahead and opened his throttle, to go streaking down the heavens at a target six thousand feet below.

Gregory had not done this for many, many years, but he had done it often in the name of glory in the murder called war. The habit was strong, and there surged up in him the savage joy of the kill. Cold meat was what he muttered over and over. Cold meat, just asking for it.

Taggart sat tensely in the rear pit. In spite of the speed of the racing dive, he lifted his head into the battering slipstream and watched with exultant face. He too could sense the helplessness of the man below, even though that man had a machine gun mounted on his bow.

The silver ship began to leap large in the ringsight. Leonard had not looked up and the dive was too swift and the silver ship's engine too loud to give him any warning.

One dive and that was all.

Gregory pressed his trips with eager thumbs and the gun before him roared, spilling flame in defiance of wind, spitting brass empties into the slipstream as the drum ate through.

Leonard saw black holes hammering into his cowl and whirled.

Gregory juggled his stick and saw the slugs eat through the young pilot's body, saw Leonard slammed down and out of sight.

Gregory pulled up with hardly another glance at the silver ship, which had begun to spin. Almost casually he sought out a broad and even spot on the river and floated his plane in to a quiet landing.

He got out and stopped to light a cigarette, to show Taggart how cool he was, and then went at an easy pace through the trees.

He came back a half hour later with a brown satchel under his arm. He waded to the pontoon and stepped up to hand the bag to Taggart.

Taggart did not look into it. He was staring at Gregory's back as the pilot slid into the front cockpit and began to start the engine with the booster.

"God," said Taggart in a whisper, as though the back of the pilot's head hypnotized him.

For three days the Tokush rolled around the bend and out into the placid width of the Arctic Sea.

And then at noon, a tan Snipe Fighter passed overhead, wheeled and dived lower, putting one wing down to go around and around. The ship snapped level, and with cut gun, Faulkner came in for a swift landing in a geyser of spray.

He taxied to the south bank and lifted himself out of the single cockpit to drop knee-deep into the water and shove the plane to an uneasy mooring.

Concernedly he struck out through the woods and at last located the splintered wreckage in the trees. For a hundred yards about were strewn fragments of the silver plane and still buckled in the broken cockpit was all the wolves had left of Leonard.

Bleakly, Streak walked about the wreckage, trying to be thorough and overlook nothing. He forced himself to make penciled notes as he went.

He found a bullet which had jammed in the seat cushion and pocketed it.

And then he dug a grave of sorts with a crooked stick and heaped stones upon the last resting place of Leonard. It was useless to mark it, except on a map. The North was accustomed to such graves.

Dismally, Streak stumbled back to the Snipe Fighter and almost blindly clambered aboard. He started the engine to run his generator and took his radiophone from the hook.

"Calling Fort Ledeau. Calling Fort Ledeau. Constable Pilot Faulkner, calling Fort Ledeau." He was trying to keep his voice steady.

"Okay," said the operator at Ledeau. "Okay, Streak, come in."

"Get me Inspector Morency."

"Okay."

For a minute he sat there, waiting, and then another voice cut in. "Constable? This is Lewis, manager of the Lucky Horseshoe. Have you found Leonard?"

"Sorry. This is police business. Get off the air." Streak knew Lewis wouldn't, didn't really care. But the habit of form was all that was taking care of him now.

"Faulkner, this is Morency. Have you found anything?"

"I've found Leonard, sir—what's left of him."

"Crashed?"

"Shot down," said Streak expressionlessly. "Shot down in one burst. I've got an intact bullet."

"And the eighteen thousand pounds?"

"The money's gone, only Leonard's receipt is left."

Morency said nothing for a long time. And then, "Have you located *him*?"

"No sign of him."

"He'll hide out after doing this—"

"He didn't do this!"

"How do you know?" said Morency.

"I . . . he couldn't . . . he wouldn't have done such a thing! Leonard didn't have a chance! He hardly knew what hit him!"

"Easy," said Morency. "Will you report back for refueling or go on to the Lucky Horseshoe?"

Lewis broke in. "He can have anything he wants up here. Anything, so long as he gets the son—"

"Off the air, Lewis," said Morency. "Look, Streak, don't

take it so hard. Keep the chin up. You've got to face it sooner or later, and I'm authorizing you to shoot him on sight. You've got a faster ship, better guns—"

"I'll handle this, sir," said Faulkner.

Morency was taken a little aback at such an answer, but he understood. "All right, Streak. Carry on." He snapped the switch shut.

"Lewis at the Lucky Horseshoe. Calling—"

"Okay, Streak. I'm still here. Listen, get that goddamn —— Dixon and I'll pay you ten thousand cash."

"I'm handling this," said Streak. "I'll get him, but in my own way."

"Don't kid yourself that he won't shoot you down," said Lewis. "After what he did to Leonard—"

"Save it," said Streak. "I'll fly in to your lake for the night and gas up."

"You bet. But get that—"

Streak hooked the phone back and shoved his throttle forward, working his ailerons to shake himself off the bar. He eased into the river and then viciously took the sky.

At White Bear Landing, as was to be expected, news of the conversation was not long in spreading. At two that afternoon, Nancy was stocking the shelves in the store when Gassy Davis hurried in. He was a Big Timber pilot, a lank Texan.

"You hear the news?" said Davis, excitedly.

Nancy's heart almost stopped beating. She turned slowly around, very white. "Have they . . . ?"

"Yeah, found Leonard. That Dixon shot him down up at

Caribou Bend on the Tokush. Didn't give him a chance. I heard Faulkner talking to Fort Ledeau, when I was coming in over Two Rivers. Shot him down and took eighteen thousand pounds! Damn him, I hope Faulkner gets the . . ." He blinked at Nancy and saw that she was trembling. "I'm sorry, ma'am. I didn't mean to scare you. I guess we'll all feel better as soon as this Dixon is gotten. Streak's flying an army Snipe, a pontoon job. It'll do two hundred and more cruising. He's got orders to shoot Dixon down on sight—"

"Please," whispered Nancy. "I . . . I think I'll . . . I've got something cooking on the stove. Excuse me."

She went into the kitchen and stood staring at the hot range, seeing a green ship flaming as it screamed in agony down the sky, seeing Bob trying to get out, feeling the frying heat and—

"NO!" she cried. "NO! They can't!"

She sank down on a chair, burying her face in her hands.

"Oh God, if there's any right in this world, don't let Streak find him. Don't—"

Suddenly she got up and straightened her calico shirt and fixed her hair. She went back into the store and saw Gassy Davis still in the doorway.

She grew cunning, and her smile was very frank. "Gassy, it would help if Streak knew where to find Dixon, wouldn't it."

"Help? Say, if you know something . . ."

"Yes, I do. I know something, but if I told it around it might reach Dixon before it got to Streak. I . . . I want to help Streak, Gassy. He . . . he and I might get married some day. . . ."

"Hell!" said Gassy Davis. "Is that so? Well I'll be . . . begging your pardon."

"Then you will help me and say nothing about it?"

"Help get Dixon? Je—I mean you bet! My God, if I could sic Streak on the right track with that Snipe . . ."

She moved closer to Gassy and smiled again. He was rather taken aback, as she had never been known to ask a favor or give any man more than the most casual word. He was overwhelmed and confused and blushed through his tan.

"Listen, Gassy," she said, pleadingly. "Streak and I made a bargain. We made up a code just in case something like this happened. He wanted the full credit. . . ."

"Sure, I know," said Gassy.

"Then listen. If something like this came up that I could help him, I was to call him at midnight any night and he'd be up and at his radiophone. You've got a Big Timber ship out there. If I could use your phone without anybody knowing, we could get Streak on the right track. If—"

"Hell, yes!" said Gassy. "Midnight? I'd stay up a dozen midnights to get that da . . . I mean Dixon. I'll meet you on the beach and you can talk Streak's ear off. Huh, I never knew the little rascal had it in him!"

"And you'll keep quiet?"

"Sure. You know me, ma'am."

"That's why I'm asking you to keep quiet."

"Okay. Midnight it is, and I hope you got the goods on Dixon's hangout. See you later."

She watched him walk down the beach to a group of miners

and pilots who were discussing the news, and she saw that Gassy was being true to his word, hanging back and saying nothing.

In a dread of apprehension lest Bob be caught this day, she went back to her blankets and counted them over and over without being able to make a tally.

"What's the matter with you?" snapped Durant, coming in. "You been at that for half an hour! What do you think I pay you forty a week for? Playing arithmetic with blankets?"

She hardly heard him. She did not know how she could get through the next nine hours.

She had not slept, but had lain for hours watching the pattern of pale moonlight upon the floor gradually edge to the log wall and then begin to climb. Every few minutes she lighted a match and looked at the dollar alarm clock on the bench beside her, which ticked loudly and interminably, seeming to pull time back with its creaking works.

At eleven-thirty she got up and silently dressed. She laced her mosquito boots and then sat looking at the dull white blur of the clock face.

The North did not approve of women smoking and so she rarely smoked, but now she found a stale package of Gold Flakes and lighted one. But something was wrong with smoking in the dark, and the tobacco had no taste. She got up and walked in silent buckskin up and down the room, to stop at last and throw the cigarette into the fireplace.

She lighted a match and saw that it was fifteen minutes until midnight. How long it had been!

Swiftly now she threw a hunting jacket over her shoulders and picked up a flashlight and crept out into the store. A board creaked and she stopped.

Suddenly Durant's door shot open and the old Scot's shoulders and head came out. He held a lantern high. "Who's that?"

"Nancy."

"What are you doing up at this time of night?" he said suspiciously. No thought of a tryst entered his head. One did not think such things of Nancy McClane.

"I couldn't sleep and I'm going to take a walk."

"Huh," snorted Durant and slammed the door. He threw it open again. "Don't make so much noise when you come in! And don't be gone long or you won't do no wor-r-rk tomorrow!" Again he slammed the door and Nancy looked at the dark rectangle of it.

She went on, taking no care about noise now. She hurried off the porch and toward the beach, running lightly, her heart beating in her throat, lest Bob Dixon fail to be listening. She could not stand another day of this.

Suddenly she stopped. Not one man, but at least twenty were there beside the canoe. And others were drifting out of the shadows toward the beach!

Gassy Davis had talked!

But she had to go through with it. She had to somehow keep them from knowing the truth. . . .

Gassy looked sheepish in the dying moonlight. "Miss Nancy, I'm sorry. I guess I had one too many. . . ."

"I asked you," said Nancy.

A bluff driller loomed beside her. "Don't mind us, Miss Nancy. We wouldn't tip off that damned Dixon if we was to be burned alive. Would we boys?"

Their chorus was ominous to Nancy.

"No harm's done," pleaded Gassy. "They think you're swell to help out. And we never knowed that you was sweet on Streak, the lucky rat!"

"Three cheers for Streak," said somebody in the crowd.

"He'll get him all right," said another.

"Name the first kid after me!" called a third. There was a crack immediately after and the speaker hit the water with a splash and sat up rubbing his jaw. "Who did that?"

"Y'ain't got no manners," growled the driller.

"Please," said Nancy. "It's almost midnight."

"I wisht I was Streak," said Gassy. "Nobody like you ever called me special. I just ride along and nobody gives a damn. . . ."

"Please," sobbed Nancy.

The plane was drifting about twenty feet from shore. The water was not deep here, and abruptly Nancy found herself picked up by the big driller. He carried her lightly and respectfully, and waded out with the water up to his thighs. He put her up in the cabin.

Some of the others came out, caught by the spirit of the thing. Gassy sloshed up to a pontoon and lifted himself up. Dripping, he eased into the cabin and sat down in his seat.

He shoved his inertia starter and the right engine caught with a protesting cough and kick.

"You . . . you are going to stay there?" said Nancy.

"Got to keep the engine going," said Gassy. He handed her the phone. "What band?"

She named the band, and he threw the switch. The phone crackled alive. She looked fearfully at Gassy. She turned and looked at the men standing up to their waists in water just outside the door.

Nervously she cleared her throat.

"Go to it," said the driller, grinning.

She started, faltered and then began to call, "Streak Faulkner. Calling Streak Faulkner. White Bear calling Streak Faulkner."

There was no answer.

"Keep going," said Gassy. "It's just midnight on the dot and sometimes you have to wiggle the dial around. Here. Give me that thing!"

He took it from her so swiftly that she could not hold it and then dared not protest. Gassy twirled the dial back and forth.

"Hey, Streak. Hey, you son of a gun, come in! Streak! Calling Streak Faulkner, you coyote. Come in, a lady wants to talk to you. Hey, Streak! Streak Faulkner! Don't make your girl sore, come in, come in."

"Let me try again," begged Nancy gripping the radiophone. She got it before Gassy could tighten his grip.

"Girl like that callin' him and he's probably snorin' someplace," complained the driller. "If I see him up at Lucky Horsehoe tomorrow, I'll give him a piece of my mind!"

"Calling Streak," said Nancy, hardly able to breathe, lest Streak himself answered, lest some mine operator happen to dial across this band.

Faintly somebody said, "Hello, hello. Okay. Come in."
But that wasn't the band!

She saw how the dial worked and she twisted it swiftly back. "Calling Streak!" she begged.

Suddenly, clear and strong, she heard Bob. "Okay. Okay, Nancy. I got it Nancy."

She controlled her tone with an effort. "Streak. You know what I mean, but they're listening."

The driller giggled, and the others nudged each other.

"What's wrong? Who is listening?" demanded Bob, up at the Big Chief Mine.

"Streak, I know where *he* is. Streak kno . . . I know where he is. Listen to me. I'm worried about you, Streak. I heard from a Big Timber pilot that Leonard of the Lucky Horseshoe had been shot down at Caribou Bend. I'm worried about you, Streak. The man who did it might get you. He might be a better machine gunner and pilot than you, Streak."

Gassy chuckled in appreciation of such concern.

She could not be sure that Bob understood and she dared not say anything directly. She must not slip. . . .

"Machine-gunned from the air. Leonard?" said Bob. "At Caribou Bend?"

"Yes. Yes! You've got your orders I know, Streak. You've got your orders to shoot *him* on sight. But you mustn't run such a risk. Oh, I know you've got a Snipe Fighter with twin Vickers. . . ."

"God," said Bob, far away at the Big Chief. "A Snipe Fighter! Does he know anything?"

"I don't think he knows, Streak. Oh, yes, I know that

eighteen hundred pounds was stolen. Yes, I know you have to shoot him on sight. But be careful, Streak."

"What shall I do?" said Bob. "I've been combing every lake in the north trying to find Taggart, and he can't be found!"

"You've got to go back to Caribou Bend," said Nancy. "Because that's on the route of the payroll planes. Listen, I know where he is, Streak, but I can't tell you here. I can't tell you here. There's still a little moonlight—two hours, perhaps. Come down and take me with you, and I'll show you. No, I can't tell because I can't show you a map. *You've got to come down here and get me.* Sure, they're listening. Yes, they're listening, but you know I love you."

"I'm starting," said Bob. "Wait for me in a canoe in the center of the lake. They'll think I'm Streak."

There was a click of a switch at the other end and Nancy dropped the phone from nerveless fingers, exhausted.

"Say," said Gassy, "that Snipe is a one-seater. He can't carry you in it."

"Must be love," said the driller. "Won't I kid Streak about this when I see him tomorrow! Take a girl for a ride in a pursuit ship! That's a hot one!"

They laughed about it, and then Gassy picked up the live radiophone and started to hang it in the bracket. He could hear a blurred voice sawing out of it and raised it to his ear.

"Nancy," Streak was calling. "Nancy. I . . ."

Gassy guffawed. "Aw, give the girl a break. If she wants to see you, she wants to see you." He hung up and threw the switch off.

Nancy was frozen. "Who . . . who was that?"

"Aw, Streak was calling you back to tell you somethin'," said Gassy. "But I says if a man won't fly a couple or three hundred miles for a ten-minute visit, he ain't no gentleman, that's what I says!"

The driller took her down from the cabin and carried her ashore. When he set her on the beach she felt sick and dizzy, but somehow she got back to the trading post. She went in and stood leaning against the closed door, staring with frightened eyes into the gloom.

She heard the crowd dispersing with more laughter and hearty good-nights, and after a while she moved to the window and looked out to see them gone.

She took Durant's Webley from the drawer and tiptoed out on the porch. The beach was deserted and she sped swiftly down to a light canoe to thrust it strongly out into the lake as she jumped in.

She dug a paddle into the luminous water, and the frail craft leaped as she drove it through the night.

CHAPTER EIGHT

BOB DIXON put one wing down and gyrated over the lake, looking carefully for a canoe out in the middle. The moon was very low and the surface of the water was like a black mirror, making it most difficult to establish. But he had ways of avoiding this curse of seaplane pilots.

With relief he sighted the craft, hardly more than a dark line. He flipped level and sped out to vertical back, cutting his gun. His wings whispered in the stillness.

The moon laid a narrow, silver path which wriggled as the small ripples from the canoe passed through it. Bob felt for the water, almost at the stalling point. Finally his pontoons touched, grabbed and plowed, and black spray was wet on his cheeks and mouth.

He taxied, locating the canoe. Nancy was driving the craft in toward him.

She took hold of a pontoon brace and stood up on it to turn and take the edge of the cockpit.

"Bob! Bob, we've got to get away quickly! Streak Faulkner answered back on that call! He's got a Snipe Fighter, ten times the ship this . . ."

Bob waited for no more. He reached down and boosted her into the rear pit. For an instant their hands and eyes met and then he turned and jabbed throttle. The ship picked up speed, got up on the step and, lightening, took the air.

Full gun, taking his course almost in the tops of tall trees, Bob raced northwest.

He had been flying for less than a minute when Nancy touched his helmet. He whirled, to see her pointing into the north, and looked closely in that direction.

A flaring streamer of red, as though a comet rode the night, was plainly seen.

It was the Snipe!

Swiftly he banked and raced due west, placing his masking fuselage between his own exhaust stack and the speeding pursuit ship. He was very low and treetops were a racing carpet, gone too swiftly to be more than a steady blur, buffeted by the ship's slipstream and challenged by the striving engine.

But Streak had seen him and Streak put the Snipe's nose down and opened the gun. To warm his Vickers, he pressed the trips.

That racketing stutter came clearly to Bob and Nancy, and the girl stared back at the flaring streamer from the Snipe's exhaust stack and saw it joined by the red pom-poms of tracer which were cutting through the Snipe's prop.

Bob wasted no time in looking. A small line of hills were under them and it was dangerous to be so low, as he could not see anything clearly. But he made out the dark maw of a canyon and lanced deeply into it, the engine thundering between the close walls.

He came out with a zoom and verticaled so swiftly that

Nancy felt crushed into the pit. Again he dived, this time across the surface of a lake, to hurdle the trees beyond.

The Snipe was still close upon him and gaining.

But now the Snipe was silhouetted by the moon, and only the ebon night was ahead of Bob. He dived anew into the hills, curving through tight valleys, bellowing over crests, and streaking down hillsides as though he had a sled and not a plane.

With inches between wingtip and ravine edge, he winged through the blackness, turning and doubling in such swift profusion that he himself was almost lost.

A level plain was ahead, and with pontoons almost sweeping the earth and slipstream blasting the grass down, he merged with the night.

When he zoomed again, the Snipe had vanished. But he did not climb. He looked about him and picked up a mountain's silhouette for guidance and, still clipping firs, raced out toward the Big Chief.

It was completely dark when he arrived over the crater, and his own marker was a light he had left burning brightly on the shore.

Nancy could not see the water or the beach, but she was not worried. It was a strange feeling she had when she was with Bob. She worried about very little. He made her feel as though she had a castle and an army of sentries.

And she need have had no concern at all, for Bob dropped a brace of flares equipped with floats, and presently the entire lake in this high crater sprang into vivid outline.

He drifted in to a smooth landing and taxied to the beach. The flares sizzled out and there was only the lantern burning upon the sand.

The engine died and the silence was deep about them. A few waves lap-lapped on the gravel, and then they too were still. They sat there quietly for minutes, saying nothing.

Finally Bob stirred himself and dropped down to a pontoon to lift Nancy out. He set her down and then moored the plane.

"I never knew how still this was," said Nancy.

"It's a friendly stillness," said Bob.

"Yes."

They walked in silence toward the log huts which were strung up the slope. But they did not go in. They sat on the steps of the first, and above them the stars were diamond dust. The north was glowing as the reduced borealis muttered, sending red and blue patterns above the horizon.

"I didn't know," said Nancy, with a sigh of pure happiness.

CHAPTER NINE

IT was a bright, warm morning and the Big Chief Mine was set in the turquoise of lake and sky touched with emerald. Bob sat in the ship, radiophone tucked into the hollow of his shoulder, listening and turning the dial, the ship's engine purring. An empty gas drum sat on the beach, part of the mine supplies, and though not the better for three years of storage, still serviceable as aviation fuel.

Nancy was putting away the breakfast dishes. She seemed to have forgotten Taggart and all the world. Indeed, as she hummed to herself moving back and forth, she was strongly tempted to go out and sit in the sun and then, if she could, convince Bob that they were out of the world and all else had best be forgotten. There was only death waiting for him if he went back, and here it was quiet, and there was game enough and stores enough to last them half a dozen lifetimes. No one would come here.

A pick with fresh earth upon it sat against the cupboard and kept getting in her way. She moved it without thinking and went on with her oddly pleasant work.

Suddenly Bob was in the doorway and she started to smile at him. But there was something in his expression which chilled her with its portent of disaster.

"Gassy Davis is going out in an hour with a payroll," said Bob deliberately. "He hasn't any guns on that machinery plane and I just heard Streak phoning Fort Ledeau saying he was flying convoy on Davis."

"But Bob! You won't—"

"What else can I do? I can't let this drag out forever. If I heard it, Taggart heard it. Taggart wouldn't stop for Streak and—"

She looked at his troubled eyes. "What do you mean?"

"Well . . ." He looked uneasy as though he was being guilty of something. "Streak thinks I'm guilty now, but . . . But he could have gotten us last night if he had tried. Faster ship, better guns. If Taggart runs into Streak, Streak will guess wrong, hold his fire. And that—I'm sorry, Nancy. Streak was my friend. I've got to go."

She threw the dish towel over the back of a chair and rolled down her sleeves and reached for her jacket. "I'm going with you."

"But Nancy—"

"If anything happened to you, I wouldn't want . . . Let's not be too hard on ourselves. If I was practical, I'd remind you that, with you gone, I would be marooned here forever!"

"That's so," said Bob, troubled. He turned and went out, and she followed him down to the ship. It was fully gassed and warmed up.

They got in without comment and Bob cast off, taxiing out into the lake. Just before he gave the throttle a shove, he looked back at the turquoise and emerald and beige of the

Big Chief Mine and then, turning, saw that Nancy was also looking. Their eyes met, both expressing the same forlorn hope.

Bob hit the throttle hard and the ship leaped ahead.

Streak was three thousand feet above Davis. There was anxiety upon his young face and he ceaselessly swept the skies and earth alertly. The lumbering machinery bimotor could not make a hundred, and so the Snipe darted back and forth in nervous zigzags to hold back and keep pace.

Now and then Streak put his thumb in the corner of his eye and looked up into the sun. The day was so bright that he could really tell nothing from the observations. And a few altocumulus furnished more cover for any waiting ship.

He was nervous, was Streak, but not because of an impending fight so much as the indecision about Bob. Last night he should have tried harder, he decided. He was soft. He couldn't follow through. But he had cut the throttle a notch and fired wide, well knowing that Bob would not land or be touched.

How could a man shoot another who had slept on the other side of a thousand lonely camps?

But he had to shoot. The path of duty was plain, and so, it seemed, was the evidence. Taggart could not fly. The green ship Bob was flying had been stolen. . . .

Unhappily Streak looked around the sky. He was soft. He couldn't pull his punch now. Bob might or might not shoot him. But Morency's orders and the evidence . . . Streak knew he would have to shoot. If Bob could bail out, all right. If not . . .

Suddenly another throb was in the air and, wildly, Streak looked up.

With the speed of light, a black ship was lancing down the sky, straight at the lumbering bimotor!

And Gregory grinned. He sat with his thumbs on his Bowden trips and held his ship in the groove with throttle wide and grinned. The Big Timber plane was in the ringsight and would stay there. Gregory could feel Taggart's eyes on his back. Taggart was afraid of these dives, afraid of this swiftly dealt death, afraid of a man so automatic in air slaughter that nothing ever went wrong. And now Taggart was frightened. There was a Snipe, the best fighting plane in the North. And in a moment that Snipe would be diving, guns going on the tail of the black plane, vastly inferior.

It amused Gregory in a bitter way. It amused him to challenge the Snipe and frighten this warped fool Taggart, a man who could shoot a voyageur in the back without a second thought, but could not stand machine-gun death in the skies. . . .

And down the groove raced the black ship, with the Big Timber plane getting bigger and bigger.

Vickers rattled somewhere far off. The Snipe was trying to warn the Big Timber pilot. Little good that would do. This was Gassy Davis' plane. Gassy Davis.

And through the top glass he could see Davis whirl about and look up, look straight through the spinning prop and ringsight, at death riding him down under hands so practiced and sure that there was no stopping it.

Too bad, thought Gregory, that he got no credit for such flying. Too bad that fool Dixon had to be blamed.

They'd given him medals for this, cried Gregory's racing thoughts. They'd given him medals and had told him he was a hero. But then it had been luckless Huns and now it was Arctic pilots. Huns for glory, but this was murder and they'd burn him if he was caught. To hell with them! They wouldn't ever catch him.

And bigger and bigger grew the bimotor.

Gassy wildly kicked rudder. He had had more warning, thanks to the Snipe, than Leonard had had.

And suddenly only the motor of the bimotor was in Gregory's sights, but he had to let drive.

The bow gun chattered, spewing oily smoke. Tracer carved straight lines through the blue, and hot lead probed into the bimotor's tanks.

One burst. Gassy was striving to bank away. But one burst of tracer had done it.

Gregory lanced by and zoomed so quickly that Taggart almost went out, through the pressure, and blood was snatched from his head.

Earth and sky churned. The bimotor exploded with a concussion which made the black ship's wings tremble.

He had gotten a Hun bomber like that once, Gregory remembered. A Hun bomber . . .

Gassy, seared by flame, fought to open his cabin. He was spinning and the earth was near. He slammed his heel under the catch. He was choking and blind with smoke. He was bleeding and battered. But he got the door open.

He plummeted out, black grip in his hand. He jerked the rip cord, and the chute streaked out and yanked him back from death.

Spinning around, he tried to see the black ship. It was above. Above and diving straight at him! Guns going!

Tracer was lacing the sky about him. Where was the Snipe?

Streak was diving. He had not had the initial speed Gregory had pulled from his altitude, but now he was the black ship's match.

The black ship was striving to kill Gassy as he drifted through the blue, helpless. Streak curbed into the rear of Gregory and Taggart and cut in the Vickers.

An astonishing thing happened. No combat pilot was Streak. No pilot with fifteen official and thirty unreported victories. No hero all bemedaled and listed as an ace.

The black ship vanished from Streak's sights as though it had dived through a hole in the sky.

Streak banked to miss tangling with Gassy's chute. Gassy waved. Gassy wasn't going three hundred and he could see. He didn't have to fly and gauge distance. . . .

Abruptly, holes appeared in Streak's cowl. He stood the Snipe on its tail and bored sky straight up. Looking up, he saw the black ship skidding into line for another burst.

Streak looped. He was an excellent pilot, but training and habit were not his. He hadn't killed threescore men in the air.

Upside down, he raced at the black ship and again Gregory was gone.

It was simple. A quick vertical, a reverse bank. Streak was just ahead and in the ringsight.

Gregory almost laughed aloud. The Snipe was a better and faster ship, with better guns, and yet the Snipe was suddenly cold meat!

He pressed the Bowdens. Tracer stripped fabric from the Snipe's rudder. The slugs inched up the turtleback toward Streak's head.

Streak reversed and verticaled. Tight on his tail came the black ship. Tracer started from the motor cowl and came swiftly back toward Streak's face.

The Snipe zoomed, climbing straight up. And for a moment it was motionless in the sights.

Gregory fired one short burst. The Snipe's engine froze with a clatter. The prop flew into a million bright fragments.

Streak felt his ship fall off on one wing. He picked speed from a whipstall and then banked again. But now he had no power. . . .

"Bob!" he yelled into the blasted skies. "Bob, for the sake of God . . . !"

Gregory was grinning. The Snipe was helpless, and now came the kill. An easy kill. Streak could not fight back without power. If he bailed out he was done and Gassy was done, and bail out he would, if this next burst failed to find his head and heart.

Gregory angled back. He was conscious of Taggart's eyes. Taggart was scared. Taggart didn't have the stomach for this methodical slaughter. Taggart was yellow at heart. A crook all his life. A yellow . . . But now for the last burst into the helpless Streak.

But it was not Gregory who fired. A shattering string of Vickers lead blotted out his panel.

With startled swiftness, Gregory swerved out of line, banked, full-gunned into a zoom, staring wildly around the sky.

He saw a green plane, a two-seater Lucky Horseshoe ship, but he knew who the pilot was.

Taggart gripped the cowl and stared at Bob's plane. He was sick with terror, was Taggart. He could not help himself. He had to depend on another man to do this fighting, this killing.

But Gregory, now that he knew, was not alarmed. This green ship was no better than his own, and he was the better pilot. Let Streak crash. There would be three kills this day but no medals. Twenty thousand pounds was reward enough.

Gregory sped straight out, to draw Bob in on the black ship's tail. This would be simple. A swift loop, a dive and the green ship would be trapped.

And Bob followed through. He sent one reassuring glance over his shoulder at Nancy. Her face was very white from what she had seen, and the speed of the dive ten thousand feet down from the sun. He gave her a grin he did not feel, but it helped her.

And then he faced front. Gregory was still racing away, straight away. There was something wrong with that. Bob had seen the cunning of the strange pilot, had seen the trick which had gotten Streak, who floundered down the sky with dead stick, toward a small lake near at hand.

Wide open, Bob blasted air in pursuit. He warmed his guns again, as it was very cold this high. He kept Gregory in the ringsight. And Gregory knew, and grinned like a sly spider. A loop, a dive, and Dixon would be cold meat.

Gregory tensed for the swift maneuver. It had worked on three Huns, the fools. It had worked, and now, on a man unexperienced in combat . . . His grin was thin and exulting and his eyes were hard behind his flashing goggles. He looked back. Straight in line. Now was the time. Now!

The black ship suddenly pulled up. Bob had been watching for something to happen but not this. The black ship had vanished!

But Bob was not afraid and so was not slow. He yanked his stick into his belt and shot skyward, standing on his rudders.

There was Gregory. Straight up at the dead point of a loop. Straight ahead, and motionless for the space of a watch tick.

It was enough.

Bob fired ahead of the black cowl with a jerk of his thumbs.

Tracer streaked and empties rattled and the Vickers chattered its savage song.

The burst was fair and Gregory raked straight through it.

The black ship fell off on one wing in a great and sickening arc.

Gregory was clutching his stomach. He brought his hand away, staring at his red and sticky fingers. He coughed and tried to focus his glance on the mad montage of heaven and earth, trees and lake, the settling Snipe and the hovering Dixon. But all was a rushing maelstrom as the black ship spun.

Gregory looked down at his hands again. He tried to move

his feet and could not. He coughed harder and blood was salty in his throat.

"He . . . he didn't . . . fall," whispered Gregory.

Suddenly he slumped.

Taggart was mad with terror. He raised up, clawing at the pilot's shoulders and finding them limp. He stared at the whirling earth all mixed with sky. The doomed scream of the yawing ship was terrifying.

He whipped off his belt and leaped.

And too late Taggart knew that he had no chute.

He was going down through miles of space, going down like a bomb, and the target was the earth. He clawed the greedy air, turning over and over. He caught flashes of the green plane, flashes of a goggled face above.

He tried to mouth an oath.

And then he knew no more.

CHAPTER TEN

"A ND so," said Morency, sitting back in his chair and looking at Bob and Streak, "when the Cree found out that Taggart was dead, he was willing to talk. Taggart had him stiff with threats and a jail looked safe in spite of the ten-year sentence for killing Hanlon. I say, he talked. And again, Dixon, I owe you an apology. You were right in connecting Taggart with the Hanlon killing, because Taggart hired that Cree to do it so that he could get what money Hanlon had left and the dust in the mine, to boot. Taggart went to White Bear and pretended innocence because he had hired the crime done and had an alibi.

"So that's twice wrong I was, Dixon. Your shooting of Taggart was definitely in the line of duty, and that intuition you always had for crime told you right."

"And now that we've established the ballistics on these machine-gun bullets and recovered the payrolls, the case is closed." He smiled a little sheepishly and then drew down his shaggy brows. "I thought you would settle it if I stirred you up enough."

But neither Streak nor Dixon smiled. They stood before the desk, unresponsive. It made Morency uncomfortable and made him talk too much.

"And as for the old judge, you heard about him? No? He

dropped dead from a heart attack. Went into a fit of temper on the bench over some petty larceny affair and went poof, out like that." He stopped again, looking worriedly at them. Suddenly he lashed out, "Why don't you say something? Don't stand there like a couple of wooden Indians, staring at me! Damn it, the case is cleared and the North is all for you, Dixon. Back in the harness again, you'll be head of the Royal Mounted in ten years. I know. I'll recommend your detachment from flying service, and you will get my job as soon as I retire. You've been on test and that—"

"I am sorry," said Dixon, levelly. "I resigned and that resignation will not be withdrawn."

"But . . . but," choked Morency. "But it's all right, Bob. It's all right! Everybody understands. I heard fifty men drink your health over at the post last night. . . ."

"I was the law because I had to be the law," said Dixon.

"I know, but—"

"And now I don't have to be the law."

"But I don't get it, old chap. I—"

"I don't need a red coat anymore," said Dixon. He softened and grinned and reached out his hand. "Inspector, you're a great little guy and I'm saving your favors for another time."

Morency limply shook his hand, bewildered.

"And as for me," said Streak, through bandages, "if that resignation of mine is still around, smooth it out and file it."

"You?" gaped Morency.

"I almost shot my best friend," said Streak. "And if orders read that way, ever, I'm done with them."

Bob turned and walked out into the compound. Nancy was

waiting there in the sunshine, and she turned to him with a smile.

"That's done," said Bob. "'Lawbook Dixon' is dead."

"And now?"

"Nancy, there's something I want to tell you. . . ."

Her look said more than words could.

"No. That's all settled," said Bob, grinning. "I even borrowed a plane for the honeymoon."

"Then is there anything else?"

"Yes. While I was up at the Big Chief, I couldn't sleep at all. And so, when I couldn't fly, I prospected those shafts."

She was afraid to speak, afraid it might not be true.

"And the bankers threw it over because there was no gold."

"Yes," whispered Nancy.

"And now, who has the title to the land?"

"Why . . . there is none. It's free for filing. . . ."

"Then let's file, and file quick!" said Bob. "The place isn't a billion-dollar mine, but there's free gold enough in the banks, and equipment enough up there, to make us at least a thousand a month the rest of our lives."

Before she could speak, Streak spoke beside them. "If I could be so rude, and if there's so much as a day laboring job. . . ."

Dixon slapped him on the back. "The manager!" And both Nancy and Streak looked at Bob Dixon. They looked at him and saw that all the hardness and false grimness was gone.

He was a kid of thirty with a rosy future to the fore, about to start on his honeymoon with a woman he knew he loved.

STORY PREVIEW

NOW that you've just ventured through one of the captivating tales in the Stories from the Golden Age collection by L. Ron Hubbard, turn the page and enjoy a preview of *Forbidden Gold*. Join daredevil pilot Kurt Reid, whose millionaire grandfather's will demands that he brave the jungles of the Yucatán and bring back a golden nugget matching one the deceased took decades before—or Kurt inherits nothing. Without options, Kurt plunges into a perilous journey, one that may kill him or reveal the love of his life.

FORBIDDEN GOLD

"THAT'S all you have to do, Mr. Reid. Just match this gold nugget and old Nathan Reid's money is yours." Kimmelmeyer looked legally at Kurt Reid and rolled the nugget in question about in his soft, plump hand.

Kurt Reid cocked his head a little on one side and took a long drag at a cigarette. Then he crossed his long legs and exhaled the smoke in a blue cloud which enveloped the desk.

Kimmelmeyer coughed, but his eyes remained very fatherly and legal. Compared to Kurt, Kimmelmeyer was small. Kimmelmeyer's head was bald, shining as though newly burnished with furniture polish. Kimmelmeyer's ears were elfinly pointed. His chin was sunk far down in a wing collar, giving his face a half-moon appearance.

"That's all I have to do," said Kurt with a twisty grin. "What's the matter, Kimmelmeyer, don't you like me any better than Nathan Reid did?"

"Like you?" gaped Kimmelmeyer, missing the point.

"You act as if I were about to go on a Sunday School picnic instead of a gold hunt in Yucatán. What if I don't want to go, huh?"

The legal look vanished. Kimmelmeyer stared amazed at Kurt. He did not feel at all at ease with this young man. Something in Kurt's attitude was vaguely insolent. The man's poise was too astounding. No, Kimmelmeyer did not understand Kurt Reid. They were too many character miles apart. Gangly, good-humored Kurt, on his part, understood Kimmelmeyer a little too well.

"But Mr. Reid!" said Kimmelmeyer. "Have you no sense of proportion at all? Here I have just offered you a chance at four million dollars and a town house and a country house and what do you do? You sit there and ask me foolish questions about whether I like you or not."

"I knew old Nathan Reid," said Kurt, dragging at his smoke. "And as certain as I'm his grandson, he didn't intend to do any good by me through you. Besides, when you're running through soup and you're out of gas and you see a landing field, it's ten to one the thing's a bog and you'll get killed anyway."

"Ai! Don't be so pessimistic. I thought all pilots were optimists."

"I'm alive," said Kurt. "Optimistic pilots are all dead."

"But what can be wrong? See here, I bring you here at my own expense—"

"At Nathan's," corrected Kurt.

"I bring you here to show you the contents of his will and you aren't even glad about it. He says right here, paragraph three, 'Whereas, if said Kurt Reid sees fit to match this gold nugget in Yucatán, I designate further that he be given my entire estate.' Now what you want, eh? You want I should just sign these papers over to you now?"

"That wouldn't be a bad idea," said Kurt. "But come along. Let's stop arguing about this thing. Does he say where this gold is down there in Yucatán?"

"No."

"Any bet he only gives me a month to find the stuff."

"That's right."

"And he makes no provision for getting me to Yucatán."

"What you want, eh?" cried Kimmelmeyer. "Can't you invest a couple thousand in return for four million?"

"Sure, but I haven't got a penny. Look here." Kurt raised his brown oxford so that Kimmelmeyer could see the sole. A hole was there, backed by a white piece of paper. "That paper is the letter you sent me," said Kurt.

"But I thought you had a good job on a transport line, eh?"

"I had one until two weeks ago. I stunted a trimotor when I was feeling good and the company didn't like it at all. In fact, they fired me. I'm flat and you'll have to give me the dough to go down there."

The request was rather sudden. Kimmelmeyer took several seconds to answer. "I . . . I'm sorry, Mr. Reid, but you see things are sort of slack and I thought . . ."

"I thought you were so hot to get me down there," said Kurt.

"Oh, I am! I am! I mean . . . er . . . should I not want to see you get all this money instead of hospitals and things maybe?"

"I don't know what the game is, Kimmelmeyer," said Kurt, squinting through the smoke, his silver-gray eyes studious. "Old Nathan Reid was my grandfather, yes, but he never liked me. He wanted me to study and follow in his footsteps, but I ran off and learned to fly. Furthermore, I was often sassy and I seem to remember telling him to go to hell once or twice. He never appreciated that, someway.

"He hated me first because I was my father's son. He hated

Dad because Dad went into the Navy and Nathan Reid was once thrown off the president's chair in Nicaragua by the United States Navy. He's got me all mixed up.

"Nathan Reid knew he could never get anything on me while he was alive. Now he's trying to do it after he's dead. He never had any scruples as a filibuster. He made enemies more than friends. After his Central American misadventures he tried to run everything by the same yardstick.

"You're just his mouthpiece, that's all. You don't know these things. I do. Nathan Reid wants to see me dead and I know damned well that a trap is waiting for me in Yucatán if I go down there looking for this gold. That pretty nugget you've got there still retains some of its quartz. That's rose quartz. The ledge is jewelry rock. Oh, I know my gold mining. If it's there, I can find it. Give me time.

"But here's something that you've never heard about. There's a saying about Yucatán and gold. The fact is known all around the Caribbean. You can look for gold in Yucatán. Gold comes out of Yucatán, brought by the Indians there. *But no white man that ever found gold in Yucatán ever got out alive except filibuster Nathan Reid.*"

"My God," whispered Kimmelmeyer.

"Nathan Reid hated me and now that he's dead he's trying to kill me. He knew that I'd go, and I'm going. I'm broke, but I'll make it some way. I know where he traveled in Yucatán. Somehow I'll get a plane and fly over his old routes there until I find the place. I'm going to beat him at his own game."

To find out more about *Forbidden Gold* and how you can obtain your copy, go to www.goldenagestories.com.

GLOSSARY

STORIES FROM THE GOLDEN AGE *reflect the words and expressions used in the 1930s and 1940s, adding unique flavor and authenticity to the tales. While a character's speech may often reflect regional origins, it also can convey attitudes common in the day. So that readers can better grasp such cultural and historical terms, uncommon words or expressions of the era, the following glossary has been provided.*

---

ailerons: hinged flaps on the trailing edge of an aircraft wing, used to control banking movements.

Bowden: a type of flexible cable used to transmit a pulling force for lighter applications over short distances.

Colt: revolver manufactured by the Colt Firearms Company, founded in 1847 by Samuel Colt (1814–1862), who revolutionized the firearms industry with the invention of the revolver.

cowl: a removable metal covering for an engine, especially an aircraft engine.

Crees: North American Indians living in central Canada.

Dominion: a self-governing territory of the British Commonwealth.

G-men: government men; agents of the Federal Bureau of Investigation.

gunwale: the upper edge of the side of a boat. Originally a gunwale was a platform where guns were mounted, and was designed to accommodate the additional stresses imposed by the artillery being used.

inertia starter: a device for starting engines. During the energizing of the starter, all movable parts within it are set in motion. After the starter has been fully energized, it is engaged to the crankshaft of the engine and the flywheel energy is transferred to the engine.

keel: a lengthwise structure along the base of a ship, and in some vessels extended downwards as a ridge to increase stability.

martinet: a rigid military disciplinarian.

mon Dieu: (French) my God.

mosquito boots: similar to riding boots, made of suede leather with thin soles.

mouthpiece: a lawyer, especially a criminal lawyer.

pannikin: a small pan, often of tin.

pitchblende: mineral occurring in brown or black pitchlike masses and containing radium.

placer: a waterborne deposit of gravel or sand containing heavy ore minerals, as gold, which have been eroded from their original bedrock and concentrated as small particles that can be washed out.

pom-poms: antiaircraft guns or their fire. The term originally applied to the Maxim automatic gun (1899–1902) from the peculiar drumming sound it made when in action.

puncheon: large timbers with one flattened side, usually used for flooring.

redcoat: an officer of the Royal Canadian Mounted Police, the federal police force of Canada.

Royal Mounted: Royal Canadian Mounted Police; federal police force of Canada.

rudder: a device used to steer ships or aircraft. A rudder is a flat plane or sheet of material attached with hinges to the craft's stern or tail. In typical aircraft, pedals operate rudders via mechanical linkages.

Russian Bear: a reference to the large brown bear, often identified with Russia itself. The bear has long been a figure in Russian folklore and has been used in decorative Russian woodcarvings, in coats of arms, etc.

Scheherazade: the female narrator of *The Arabian Nights,* who during one thousand and one adventurous nights saved her life by entertaining her husband, the king, with stories.

slipstream: the airstream pushed back by a revolving aircraft propeller.

snap-brim: a felt hat with a dented crown, and the brim turned up in back and down in front.

Snipe Fighter: British single-seat fighter biplane armed with a set of twin front-mounted Vickers machine guns.

tracer: a bullet or shell whose course is made visible by a trail of flames or smoke, used to assist in aiming.

turtleback: the part of the airplane behind the cockpit that is shaped like the back of a turtle.

Union Jack: a national flag of the United Kingdom. Canada was colonized by the French and British. In 1763 England gained possession of the French territory by treaty and Canada came to be dominated by the British until the country attained independence in 1931.

Vassar: a women's college founded in 1861 and one of the oldest institutions of higher education in the US. It was associated in its early years with the social elite and upper class.

Vickers: a machine gun made for the British Army by a company called Vickers Limited. The gun had a reputation for great solidity and reliability.

voyageur: a boatman, woodsman, trapper or explorer formerly hired by fur companies to carry furs and supplies from one remote station to another, especially in Canada and the Northwestern US.

Webley: Webley and Scott handgun; an arms manufacturer based in England that produced handguns from 1834. Webley is famous for the revolvers and automatic pistols it supplied to the British Empire's military, particularly the British Army, from 1887 through both World War I and World War II.

whipstall: a maneuver in a small aircraft in which it goes into a vertical climb, pauses briefly, and then drops toward the earth, nose first.

wing collar: a shirt collar, used especially in men's formal clothing, in which the front edges are folded down in such a way as to resemble a pair of wings.

wooden Indians: carved wooden figures of Native Americans, formerly used as advertisements outside tobacco shops.

Yank: Yankee; term used to refer to Americans in general.

Yucatán: a peninsula mostly in southeastern Mexico between the Caribbean Sea and the Gulf of Mexico.

L. Ron Hubbard
in the Golden Age
of Pulp Fiction

*In writing an adventure story
a writer has to know that he is adventuring
for a lot of people who cannot.
The writer has to take them here and there
about the globe and show them
excitement and love and realism.
As long as that writer is living the part of an
adventurer when he is hammering
the keys, he is succeeding with his story.*

*Adventuring is a state of mind.
If you adventure through life, you have a
good chance to be a success on paper.*

*Adventure doesn't mean globe-trotting,
exactly, and it doesn't mean great deeds.
Adventuring is like art.
You have to live it to make it real.*

—L. RON HUBBARD

L. Ron Hubbard
and American
Pulp Fiction

B ORN March 13, 1911, L. Ron Hubbard lived a life at least as expansive as the stories with which he enthralled a hundred million readers through a fifty-year career.

Originally hailing from Tilden, Nebraska, he spent his formative years in a classically rugged Montana, replete with the cowpunchers, lawmen and desperadoes who would later people his Wild West adventures. And lest anyone imagine those adventures were drawn from vicarious experience, he was not only breaking broncs at a tender age, he was also among the few whites ever admitted into Blackfoot society as a bona fide blood brother. While if only to round out an otherwise rough and tumble youth, his mother was that rarity of her time—a thoroughly educated woman—who introduced her son to the classics of Occidental literature even before his seventh birthday.

But as any dedicated L. Ron Hubbard reader will attest, his world extended far beyond Montana. In point of fact, and as the son of a United States naval officer, by the age of eighteen he had traveled over a quarter of a million miles. Included therein were three Pacific crossings to a then still mysterious Asia, where he ran with the likes of Her British Majesty's agent-in-place

for North China, and the last in the line of Royal Magicians from the court of Kublai Khan. For the record, L. Ron Hubbard was also among the first Westerners to gain admittance to forbidden Tibetan monasteries below Manchuria, and his photographs of China's Great Wall long graced American geography texts.

L. Ron Hubbard, left, at Congressional Airport, Washington, DC, 1931, with members of George Washington University flying club.

Upon his return to the United States and a hasty completion of his interrupted high school education, the young Ron Hubbard entered George Washington University. There, as fans of his aerial adventures may have heard, he earned his wings as a pioneering barnstormer at the dawn of American aviation. He also earned a place in free-flight record books for the longest sustained flight above Chicago. Moreover, as a roving reporter for *Sportsman Pilot* (featuring his first professionally penned articles), he further helped inspire a generation of pilots who would take America to world airpower.

Immediately beyond his sophomore year, Ron embarked on the first of his famed ethnological expeditions, initially to then untrammeled Caribbean shores (descriptions of which would later fill a whole series of West Indies mystery-thrillers). That the Puerto Rican interior would also figure into the future of Ron Hubbard stories was likewise no accident. For in addition to cultural studies of the island, a 1932–33

LRH expedition is rightly remembered as conducting the first complete mineralogical survey of a Puerto Rico under United States jurisdiction.

There was many another adventure along this vein: As a lifetime member of the famed Explorers Club, L. Ron Hubbard charted North Pacific waters with the first shipboard radio direction finder, and so pioneered a long-range navigation system universally employed until the late twentieth century. While not to put too fine an edge on it, he also held a rare Master Mariner's license to pilot any vessel, of any tonnage in any ocean.

Yet lest we stray too far afield, there is an LRH note at this juncture in his saga, and it reads in part:

"I started out writing for the pulps, writing the best I knew, writing for every mag on the stands, slanting as well as I could."

To which one might add: His earliest submissions date from the summer of 1934, and included tales drawn from true-to-life Asian adventures, with characters roughly modeled on British/American intelligence operatives he had known in Shanghai. His early Westerns were similarly peppered with details drawn from personal experience. Although therein lay a first hard lesson from the often cruel world of the pulps. His first Westerns were soundly rejected as lacking the authenticity of a Max Brand yarn

Capt. L. Ron Hubbard in Ketchikan, Alaska, 1940, on his Alaskan Radio Experimental Expedition, the first of three voyages conducted under the Explorers Club flag.

(a particularly frustrating comment given L. Ron Hubbard's Westerns came straight from his Montana homeland, while Max Brand was a mediocre New York poet named Frederick Schiller Faust, who turned out implausible six-shooter tales from the terrace of an Italian villa).

Nevertheless, and needless to say, L. Ron Hubbard persevered and soon earned a reputation as among the most publishable names in pulp fiction, with a ninety percent placement rate of first-draft manuscripts. He was also among the most prolific, averaging between seventy and a hundred thousand words a month. Hence the rumors that L. Ron Hubbard had redesigned a typewriter for faster keyboard action and pounded out manuscripts on a continuous roll of butcher paper to save the precious seconds it took to insert a single sheet of paper into manual typewriters of the day.

That all L. Ron Hubbard stories did not run beneath said byline is yet another aspect of pulp fiction lore. That is, as publishers periodically rejected manuscripts from top-drawer authors if only to avoid paying top dollar, L. Ron Hubbard and company just as frequently replied with submissions under various pseudonyms. In Ron's case, the list

A MAN OF MANY NAMES

Between 1934 and 1950, L. Ron Hubbard authored more than fifteen million words of fiction in more than two hundred classic publications. To supply his fans and editors with stories across an array of genres and pulp titles, he adopted fifteen pseudonyms in addition to his already renowned L. Ron Hubbard byline.

Winchester Remington Colt
Lt. Jonathan Daly
Capt. Charles Gordon
Capt. L. Ron Hubbard
Bernard Hubbel
Michael Keith
Rene Lafayette
Legionnaire 148
Legionnaire 14830
Ken Martin
Scott Morgan
Lt. Scott Morgan
Kurt von Rachen
Barry Randolph
Capt. Humbert Reynolds

included: Rene Lafayette, Captain Charles Gordon, Lt. Scott Morgan and the notorious Kurt von Rachen—supposedly on the lam for a murder rap, while hammering out two-fisted prose in Argentina. The point: While L. Ron Hubbard as Ken Martin spun stories of Southeast Asian intrigue, LRH as Barry Randolph authored tales of

L. Ron Hubbard, circa 1930, at the outset of a literary career that would finally span half a century.

romance on the Western range—which, stretching between a dozen genres is how he came to stand among the two hundred elite authors providing close to a million tales through the glory days of American Pulp Fiction.

In evidence of exactly that, by 1936 L. Ron Hubbard was literally leading pulp fiction's elite as president of New York's American Fiction Guild. Members included a veritable pulp hall of fame: Lester "Doc Savage" Dent, Walter "The Shadow" Gibson, and the legendary Dashiell Hammett—to cite but a few.

Also in evidence of just where L. Ron Hubbard stood within his first two years on the American pulp circuit: By the spring of 1937, he was ensconced in Hollywood, adopting a Caribbean thriller for Columbia Pictures, remembered today as *The Secret of Treasure Island.* Comprising fifteen thirty-minute episodes, the L. Ron Hubbard screenplay led to the most profitable matinée serial in Hollywood history. In accord with Hollywood culture, he was thereafter continually called

The 1937 Secret of Treasure Island, *a fifteen-episode serial adapted for the screen by L. Ron Hubbard from his novel,* Murder at Pirate Castle.

upon to rewrite/doctor scripts—most famously for long-time friend and fellow adventurer Clark Gable.

In the interim—and herein lies another distinctive chapter of the L. Ron Hubbard story—he continually worked to open Pulp Kingdom gates to up-and-coming authors. Or, for that matter, anyone who wished to write. It was a fairly unconventional stance, as markets were already thin and competition razor sharp. But the fact remains, it was an L. Ron Hubbard hallmark that he vehemently lobbied on behalf of young authors—regularly supplying instructional articles to trade journals, guest-lecturing to short story classes at George Washington University and Harvard, and even founding his own creative writing competition. It was established in 1940, dubbed the Golden Pen, and guaranteed winners both New York representation and publication in *Argosy*.

But it was John W. Campbell Jr.'s *Astounding Science Fiction* that finally proved the most memorable LRH vehicle. While every fan of L. Ron Hubbard's galactic epics undoubtedly knows the story, it nonetheless bears repeating: By late 1938, the pulp publishing magnate of Street & Smith was determined to revamp *Astounding Science Fiction* for broader readership. In particular, senior editorial director F. Orlin Tremaine called for stories with a stronger *human element*. When acting editor John W. Campbell balked, preferring his spaceship-driven tales,

Tremaine enlisted Hubbard. Hubbard, in turn, replied with the genre's first truly *character-driven* works, wherein heroes are pitted not against bug-eyed monsters but the mystery and majesty of deep space itself—and thus was launched the Golden Age of Science Fiction.

The names alone are enough to quicken the pulse of any science fiction aficionado, including LRH friend and protégé, Robert Heinlein, Isaac Asimov, A. E. van Vogt and Ray Bradbury. Moreover, when coupled with LRH stories of fantasy, we further come to what's rightly been described as the foundation of every modern tale of horror: L. Ron Hubbard's immortal *Fear*. It was rightly proclaimed by Stephen King as one of the very few works to genuinely warrant that overworked term "classic"—as in: *"This is a classic tale of creeping, surreal menace and horror. . . . This is one of the really, really good ones."*

L. Ron Hubbard, 1948, among fellow science fiction luminaries at the World Science Fiction Convention in Toronto.

To accommodate the greater body of L. Ron Hubbard fantasies, Street & Smith inaugurated *Unknown*—a classic pulp if there ever was one, and wherein readers were soon thrilling to the likes of *Typewriter in the Sky* and *Slaves of Sleep* of which Frederik Pohl would declare: *"There are bits and pieces from Ron's work that became part of the language in ways that very few other writers managed."*

And, indeed, at J. W. Campbell Jr.'s insistence, Ron was regularly drawing on themes from the Arabian Nights and

105

so introducing readers to a world of genies, jinn, Aladdin and Sinbad—all of which, of course, continue to float through cultural mythology to this day.

At least as influential in terms of post-apocalypse stories was L. Ron Hubbard's 1940 *Final Blackout*. Generally acclaimed as the finest anti-war novel of the decade and among the ten best works of the genre ever authored—here, too, was a tale that would live on in ways few other writers imagined. Hence, the later Robert Heinlein verdict: "Final Blackout *is as perfect a piece of science fiction as has ever been written.*"

Like many another who both lived and wrote American pulp adventure, the war proved a tragic end to Ron's sojourn in the pulps. He served with distinction in four theaters and was highly decorated for commanding corvettes in the North Pacific. He was also grievously wounded in combat, lost many a close friend and colleague and thus resolved to say farewell to pulp fiction and devote himself to what it had supported these many years—namely, his serious research.

Portland, Oregon, 1943; L. Ron Hubbard captain of the US Navy subchaser PC 815.

But in no way was the LRH literary saga at an end, for as he wrote some thirty years later, in 1980:

"Recently there came a period when I had little to do. This was novel in a life so crammed with busy years, and I decided to amuse myself by writing a novel that was pure science fiction."

106

That work was *Battlefield Earth: A Saga of the Year 3000*. It was an immediate *New York Times* bestseller and, in fact, the first international science fiction blockbuster in decades. It was not, however, L. Ron Hubbard's magnum opus, as that distinction is generally reserved for his next and final work: The 1.2 million word *Mission Earth*.

> **Final Blackout**
> *is as perfect a piece of science fiction as has ever been written.*
>
> —Robert Heinlein

How he managed those 1.2 million words in just over twelve months is yet another piece of the L. Ron Hubbard legend. But the fact remains, he did indeed author a ten-volume *dekalogy* that lives in publishing history for the fact that each and every volume of the series was also a *New York Times* bestseller.

Moreover, as subsequent generations discovered L. Ron Hubbard through republished works and novelizations of his screenplays, the mere fact of his name on a cover signaled an international bestseller. . . . Until, to date, sales of his works exceed hundreds of millions, and he otherwise remains among the most enduring and widely read authors in literary history. Although as a final word on the tales of L. Ron Hubbard, perhaps it's enough to simply reiterate what editors told readers in the glory days of American Pulp Fiction:

He writes the way he does, brothers, because he's been there, seen it and done it!

THE STORIES FROM THE GOLDEN AGE

Your ticket to adventure starts here with the Stories from the Golden Age collection by master storyteller L. Ron Hubbard. These gripping tales are set in a kaleidoscope of exotic locales and brim with fascinating characters, including some of the most vile villains, dangerous dames and brazen heroes you'll ever get to meet.

The entire collection of over one hundred and fifty stories is being released in a series of eighty books and audiobooks. For an up-to-date listing of available titles, go to www.goldenagestories.com.

AIR ADVENTURE

FAR-FLUNG ADVENTURE

SEA ADVENTURE

TALES FROM THE ORIENT

MYSTERY

FANTASY

Borrowed Glory	*If I Were You*
The Crossroads	*The Last Drop*
Danger in the Dark	*The Room*
The Devil's Rescue	*The Tramp*
He Didn't Like Cats	

SCIENCE FICTION

The Automagic Horse	*A Matter of Matter*
Battle of Wizards	*The Obsolete Weapon*
Battling Bolto	*One Was Stubborn*
The Beast	*The Planet Makers*
Beyond All Weapons	*The Professor Was a Thief*
A Can of Vacuum	*The Slaver*
The Conroy Diary	*Space Can*
The Dangerous Dimension	*Strain*
Final Enemy	*Tough Old Man*
The Great Secret	*240,000 Miles Straight Up*
Greed	*When Shadows Fall*
The Invaders	

WESTERN

Charge into all the Action!

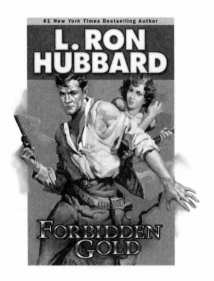

The Yucatán jungle hides a world of secrets... of wealth, love and fate. Daredevil pilot Kurt Reid is about to fly into the heart of it in search of his destiny—and gold. It's an adventure as daring and dangerous as any undertaken by Indiana Jones. Thanks to his grandfather's dying wish, his entire inheritance hangs on his finding one particular gold nugget. Before it's over, he'll either land on a Mayan sacrificial altar or in the arms of his sexy copilot Joy. One way or another, things are heating up fast.

Journey into the heart of darkness in the Mexican rain forest as the audio version of *Forbidden Gold* takes you to a place where the glitter of gold makes passions seethe.

Get
Forbidden Gold

PAPERBACK: $9.95 OR AUDIOBOOK: $12.95 EACH
Free Shipping & Handling for Book Club Members
CALL TOLL-FREE: 1-877-8GALAXY (1-877-842-5299)
OR GO ONLINE TO **www.goldenagestories.com**

Galaxy Press, 7051 Hollywood Blvd., Suite 200, Hollywood, CA 90028

JOIN THE PULP REVIVAL
America in the 1930s and 40s

Pulp fiction was in its heyday and 30 million readers were regularly riveted by the larger-than-life tales of master storyteller L. Ron Hubbard. For this was pulp fiction's golden age, when the writing was raw and every page packed a walloping punch.

That magic can now be yours. An evocative world of nefarious villains, exotic intrigues, courageous heroes and heroines—a world that today's cinema has barely tapped for tales of adventure and swashbucklers.

Enroll today in the Stories from the Golden Age Club and begin receiving your monthly feature edition selected from more than 150 stories in the collection.

You may choose to enjoy them as either a paperback or audiobook for the special membership price of $9.95 each month along with FREE shipping and handling.

CALL TOLL-FREE: 1-877-8GALAXY
(1-877-842-5299) OR GO ONLINE TO
www.goldenagestories.com
AND BECOME PART OF THE PULP REVIVAL!

Prices are set in US dollars only. For non-US residents, please call
1-323-466-7815 for pricing information. Free shipping available for US residents only.

Galaxy Press, 7051 Hollywood Blvd., Suite 200, Hollywood, CA 90028